EYE FOR AN EYE

She was pretty far gone. Not as far as she was going to go, though. She hobbled along the trail for a few paces. A shot sounded. She fell down.

A ragged scarecrow figure perched on the edge of the clifftop, to the right of the cleft. His rifle pointed downward at the fallen girl. A puff of gunsmoke smudged the air in front of him. He hadn't seen Boyd.

With one smooth, instinctive motion, Boyd shouldered the carbine and fired. He didn't have to think about it, he just did it. The weapon barked, a sharp flat cracking report.

Scarecrow Man fell backward, out of sight.

When Boyd shot at something, he hit it. That was why he was here . . .

McMASTERS
VIOLENT SUNDAY

Lee Morgan

J

JOVE BOOKS, NEW YORK

VIOLENT SUNDAY

A Jove Book / published by arrangement with
the author

PRINTING HISTORY
Jove edition / April 1996

The Putnam Berkley World Wide Web site address is
http://www.berkley.com

ISBN: 0-515-11842-7

A JOVE BOOK®
Jove Books are published by The Berkley Publishing Group,
200 Madison Avenue, New York, New York 10016.
JOVE and the "J" design are trademarks
belonging to Jove Publications, Inc.

PRINTED IN THE UNITED STATES OF AMERICA

10 9 8 7 6 5 4 3 2 1

One

Boyd McMasters was manhunting when he saw the girl.

It was a little past noon on an early May day in Montana, 1882. Boyd was on a mountain trail, riding a gray horse. Tied behind it was a packhorse. On the right was a rocky cliff face, on the left a sheer five-hundred-foot drop. Between: a narrow trail.

Boyd's horse was blindfolded, a kerchief knotted carefully over its eyes. So was the packhorse. This was to keep them from being spooked by the big nothingness yawning only a misstep away. They plodded along, hooves sinking into the soft claylike ground. The trail ribboned up the cliffside, winding along the curves, climbing ever upward. The sky was bright blue. The sun was high, sparkling. The temperature was about forty-five degrees Fahrenheit. In the high mountain valleys between the Belt Mountains and the East Rockies, spring had just begun.

Boyd was long, lean, wiry. His hat marked him as

an outlander. Not the stylishly pinched, high-crowned type characteristic of the Northern Range, it was low-crowned, flat, wide-brimmed, a product of the Southwest. Boyd was from Texas. He'd be damned if he'd get a new hat just to go on a manhunt in Montana.

The hat was tied down tight, protection against the winds gusting through the canyon. His jacket was inside a saddlebag. After a night of subfreezing cold, the sun felt good. He wore a dark green long-sleeved shirt, wrist-length rancher's gloves, brown pants, boots. He was dirty—two day's and a night's worth. Against his grimy face, his eyes were startlingly bright, white. Restless, in constant motion, they scanned the scene.

Slung to the saddle, on the left side of the horse, was a long rifle, rigged butt upright in the scabbard. Outlined against its protective sheath, it resembled a buffalo gun. It was six feet long, not easily unlimbered for fast action. For that, Boyd was armed with a carbine, a short, accurate saddle gun. Also, a pair of holstered Colts. And a knife. He was dirty, but the weapons were clean, spotless.

The horse stumbled. Boyd's blood ran cold. A stone shot out from under a hoof, sailing over the edge into space. The sudden lurch gave Boyd a glimpse of the long drop.

The horse found its footing, recovered. Boyd leaned toward the cliff, away from the abyss. He couldn't see the drop now. The edge was in his way.

He listened for the sound of the rock hitting bottom, didn't hear it. He thought he'd missed it.

From below came a distant clatter.

Boyd realized that he was holding his breath, let it out. He patted the horse's neck, made soothing sounds. The animal slogged onward, upward, uncomplaining.

Boyd looked back, to make sure the packhorse was okay. It was.

The ascent continued. The cliff was the north wall of a canyon deep in the Blue Pine Hills. Hills? Most other places, each hill would have been considered a fairly good-sized mountain, but not here. Not in Montana.

The slopes were covered with pine trees. Not the cliff, of course. Only dwarf pines and bushes sprouted from its sheer rock face. But the surrounding hills were thickly forested, their foliage not blue but silvery gray-green. Their resinous pine scent peppered the cool, fresh air.

In all directions, as far as the eye could see, there was no sign of human habitation.

A few birds of prey wheeled through the heights, soaring on the thermals.

A cloud covered the sun. The sudden chill made Boyd shiver.

The canyon ran east-west. Ahead, the cliff trail rose east for another hundred yards or so, before vanishing around a blind curve.

The cloud passed over the face of the sun. The shadow veil lifted, bringing a return of welcome warmth.

Other clouds, white and fleecy, rolled across the sky. Not storm clouds, for which Boyd kept a wary eye. Up here, May didn't mean a damn. Under the trees, snow was on the ground, and the nights were below freezing. A sudden snowstorm now could kill a man as dead as one in December.

But spring was in the air. Moist earth smells told of the quickening. Tender shoots, grassy green, thrust out from cracks in the cliff wall. Here and there were patches of wildflowers, yellow, white, and blue, their heads no bigger than baby peas.

Projecting rocks cast shadows on the trail. Gnats swarmed in the sunlight. Boyd passed through bands of light and shade.

The trail narrowed as it neared the curve. Boyd got down from the saddle. Reins in hand, he started forward on foot, horses following.

The gray's ears pricked. There was a sound of a rockfall, coming from somewhere on the other side of the blind corner.

Boyd stopped.

It wasn't much of a rockfall by the sound of it, just a few loose stones clattering downslope, bouncing off ledges.

Boyd unslung the carbine.

Rockfall sounds faded, swallowed up by the canyon. Boyd waited, motionless. The sounds were not repeated.

After a while, Boyd started forward. In one hand he held the carbine, leveled waist high. In the other, he held the reins, trailing behind him.

Bushes grew out of the side of the cliff. One had a woody main stem as thick as Boyd's arm. He tested it. It was solidly rooted. He hitched the reins to it.

The gray brushed against the bush, nuzzled it, and began munching on it. The packhorse, similarly blindfolded, soon found something on which to browse.

Fifty feet away lay the blind curve. Boyd went to it, walking soft.

He peeked around the corner.

The cliff was a curtain with folds in it, a stone curtain. Beyond the outswelling curve, the wall arched inward, sweeping in a slow, gentle concavity for a few hundred yards before the next bend. The trail followed it. At its center was a V-shaped gap. The trail vanished at the base of the cleft, reappearing on the other side. The notch fanned upward to the cliff top.

Once, a massive outcropping had jutted out from the rock wall. It had fallen ages ago, leaving a wedge-shaped seam. At the bottom of the cleft, a fan of loose dirt and boulders spilled into the canyon floor.

The cleft was deep, tree-lined, with thick underbrush.

A line appeared at the top of the fan, drawn in the dirt by a falling rock. Boyd's eye followed the line, tracing it upward to its point of origin, where the rock had emerged from the cleft.

Something was moving in the underbrush, near the point of the V.

A flash of white showed through the trees. There was snow on the ground, but this wasn't it. This was moving. It was hard to see, through the thicket.

He lost sight of it for a moment. It continued to dislodge small stones, sending them tumbling downhill, allowing him to trace its passage. It moved toward the left, a ghostly white form.

It broke out of the bushes at the edge of the cleft, stumbling into view. A human figure, slight, slender, naked.

A woman—no, a girl. She had long, stringy yellow hair. Her flesh was yellow-white, like old bone. Mud-streaked. Covered from head to toe with cuts and bruises.

Her body was stiff, angular, contorted. She moved jerkily, like a sleepwalker. She was at the extremes of exhaustion and endurance.

She rose up from between the bushes, starting across a stony patch of ground between the cleft and the trail. Bent double, almost on her hands and knees, she crossed slantwise down the slope.

She slipped, falling heavily. She slid face down across the rocks for fifteen feet or so before coming to a stop.

The trail was near. She crawled to it on hands and knees, then tried to rise. It was painful to watch, reminding Boyd of a half-squashed bug whose limbs are still twitching.

Boyd wanted to call out to her but was afraid to do so. She looked crazed. A sudden shout from a stranger might cause her to do God-knows-what. Throw herself off the cliff, maybe . . . She was pretty far gone.

Not as far as she was going to be, though.

She hobbled along the trail for a few paces. A shot sounded. She fell down.

A second shot sounded, hard on the heels of the first, following it so closely that it might have been taken for an echo.

It was fired by Boyd, at the girl's killer.

She was dead, no doubt about it. He'd made enough kills himself to know that. It had all happened so fast. From the time she had first broken cover to the time when the first shot rang out had been little more than sixty seconds.

Boyd had been so dumbstruck by the apparition that he'd failed to pay proper attention to his surroundings. His constant scanning of the landscape had stopped while his eyes were fixed on her.

Then, the shot. A ragged scarecrow figure perched on the edge of the clifftop, to the right of the cleft. His rifle pointed downward at the fallen girl. A puff of gunsmoke smudged the air in front of him. He hadn't seen Boyd.

With one smooth, instinctive motion, Boyd shouldered the carbine and fired. He didn't have to think about it, he just did it. The weapon barked, a sharp, flat, cracking report.

Scarecrow Man fell backward, out of sight.

When Boyd shot at something, he hit it. That was why he was here.

But whom had he shot?

Scarecrow Man lay sprawled on the ground, a few feet away from the cliff edge. His horse nuzzled him.

It was the damnedest nag, a coal-black mare with a long, shaggy, charcoal-gray mane. Gaunt, with its ribs showing. Black triangular ears stood up on the top of its head like spear points. It danced around the corpse, pawing the ground with its front hoofs.

The mare lifted its snout, red with gore. It pawed the corpse's chest, trampling the area of the entry wound. Its head dipped, tongue greedily slurping fresh blood.

Damn!

Boyd crouched behind some bushes at the top of the cleft. He must have grunted with involuntary disgust, for the horse jerked its head up, looking straight where he was hiding.

Its eyes were moist, reddish-brown orbs, the color of dried blood. Wild, glowing. The blood smeared on its snout was bright red.

The horse turned, ran away.

Boyd was tempted to put a bullet in it, ending its unnatural existence. A horse that drank blood—!

He held his fire. That galloping nightmare was more useful alive than dead.

Still, he was shaken. Violent death he was used to, but not this. Horses were grazing animals, alien to a taste for blood. This went beyond the natural order of things.

He stayed put, under cover, scanning the scene.

He was at the edge of a plateau, or park, as these high mountain valleys were called. Oval-shaped tableland, its long axis running east-west for several miles. In its center was a still blue lake. The far side of the park was bordered by dark forests, rising into peaks, and beyond them still higher peaks. In the northern distance lay a sawtooth blue mountain range.

Boyd, a stranger here, knew where he was. In his head he carried a mental map of the locality, branded into his memory after much study of charts and maps, rounded out by close questioning of the locals.

The round, almost circular, lake could only be Skyfall Lake, its shape reputedly owed to a crater caused by an eons-ago meteor strike. Its waters were sapphire-blue. What looked like a sawtooth mountain range was in reality one mountain: Wendigo Mountain, huge, multi-peaked.

In a sense, the Blue Pine Hills were foothills of the mighty mountain, falling away from it in terraces to the south in a loose, U-shaped landform. Running parallel to it on the flat was Ripsaw River, fast and deep. Along the river's south bank was a branch line of the NIRR, the Northern Range Rail Road.

Northwest of the hills, up the line, lay the whistlestop town of Blue Pine. Boyd had entered the hills from the west. At their center was the park with the lake. East, beyond the far side of the hills, was Sun Dog junction, a vital shipping point for the region's cattle ranchers.

River, railroad, flat, and towns—all were now lost from view, hidden by the brooding hills. In all directions: wilderness.

The nightmare horse angled across the park, its course taking it east of the lake. There were few trees; most were charred, lightning-blasted. They stuck out of the ground like blackened bones. Winds blew across the open space.

The ground was pretty much bare of snow, though a few patches remained in the hollows, scuds of dirty-white foam. It was covered with short, thick grass, tough, matted, waxy, the color of dead straw. The turf was wet and spongy, good for tracks and footprints.

Boyd stayed low, not skylining. The only sign of life in the park was the horse. Boyd stayed low anyway.

The horse dwindled in the distance.

Boyd circled to the right, following the rim of the cleft, sheltering below it. He wanted a look at the corpse.

He smelled it first. Violent death has its own peculiar stink of blood, shit, and piss. That was there, mixed with a sour reek of unwashed human flesh. Scarecrow Man had stunk long before the fatal bullet had ended sphincter control.

Boyd, downwind, got a faceful of the stench and wrinkled his nostrils in disgust.

Talk about a two-legged skunk—! Whew!

Parting the bushes in front of his face, he took a closer view.

Scarecrow Man? Hell, he looked like a damned mountain man! All ragged buckskins and hair . . .

He lay flat on his back, as if the bullet through his chest had nailed him to the ground. His rifle lay nearby. He didn't look like much, mostly skin, hair, and bones. Long hair, long as a woman's, greasy and matted with filth. Wispy pointed beard, reaching down to his chest. His chest was a bloody ruin from the trampling, but underneath it all could still be seen the entry wound from Boyd's bullet.

Crude buckskins, shirt and breeches, were grimy black. But the rifle was new, and well kept.

Bony face, wizened, with jutting cheekbones and sunken eyes and cheeks. Eyes and mouth were open.

He looked mad as hell about being dead.

The stink was so strong, Boyd could taste it. He covered mouth and nose with his bandanna. It helped, but not much.

The horse was a speck in the distance. Boyd rose from his place of concealment, approaching the corpse.

Sign told the tale. A single set of footprints stretched across the clifftop, angling back from the lip of the cleft northeast to a place at the middle distance at the edge of the woods. Bare footprints. The girl's.

There was blood in the tracks and some toes were missing.

The place where she had emerged from the woods seemed to be a solid screen of foliage, but somewhere in the thicket was a trail.

Close behind the fugitive was Scarecrow Man. His horse's tracks emerged from the same hidden trail, paralleling the footprints. He followed them to the cliff, dismounted, saw her making her way along the cliffside path, and shot her. He didn't see Boyd, who shot him. The horse trampled the dead man and ran.

The dead man had pointed teeth.

At first Boyd thought his eyes were playing tricks,

so he took a closer look. Flies buzzed the corpse. Stench poured from its mouth and from its other holes: asshole and bullethole.

Sure enough, the teeth were pointed. Not just the canines but both sets of uppers and lowers. They hadn't grown that way. They'd been filed.

Beady-eyed, with a mouthful of sharp, pointed teeth, Scarecrow looked like a weasel. No, a possum. A dead one.

Boyd shivered, not from fear. Cold winds blew hard, gusting down from the north. The chill cut to the bone. He missed his jacket, back in the saddlebag. His hands were gloved, warm, holding the carbine level.

The horse was gone, vanished while Boyd was eyeing Scarecrow. It disappeared in the vicinity of the place at woods' edge from which it originally had emerged. No doubt it was now on the hidden trail, retracing its path, heading home.

At that home, who—*what*—was waiting?

Boyd missed his binoculars. They were in the saddlebags too. There hadn't been time to grab them, or any other niceties, when the first shot had sounded. He'd dropped his man and started up the cleft, zigzagging upward, dodging from cover to cover. Not until he'd reached the clifftop did he learn that Scarecrow was alone.

Maybe he had partners following behind, farther back along the trail. Or maybe not. A fellow with teeth filed to a point might not be too sociable. If he had partners, though, that would be one hell of an outfit.

One hell of an outfit.

No longer could Boyd ignore the cold. The sun was still out, but the temperature had dropped ten degrees in as many minutes.

A cloud was rising in the north—huge, towering, slate-gray with purple edges. The top of Mount Wendigo was already hidden from view. The cloud came on, rolling, boiling, churning. Clawing for the heights, the zenith.

Storm cloud.

"Damn," Boyd said, then, with feeling, "Damn!"

Up here, a storm meant snow. There went his plan to follow the tracks back to Scarecrow's lair, somewhere there in the pines. Snow would cover those tracks. Being caught in a snowstorm would be no picnic, either.

Too bad, but that was the way of it. No sense arguing with a fact. With luck, he could be at the bottom of the cliff trail before the storm broke.

He wanted Scarecrow. That body could prove useful. The easy way would be to just take the head, using his knife to sever it at the neck.

That wasn't the kind of behavior the Cattleman's Protective Association expected of its agents.

Not officially, anyhow.

Which meant that Scarecrow had to arrive more or less intact. Working quickly, Boyd cut and trimmed a pair of eight-foot-long saplings, using vines to tie them together at one end. There was a rope looped to his saddle, but he didn't want to take the time to get it and come back. The vines were brown and tough but supple. The poles made a V-shape. To the ends of them he tied a three-foot branch, the base of the triangle. A pair of crosspieces were secured to the framework at right angles. He worked hard, his back to the wind.

Now he had a travois, a crude but workable carrier. He would tie the corpse to it and be on his way.

Strung on a thong hanging from Scarecrow's neck was a greasy, wallet-size, rawhide pouch. It had been worn inside his shirt until the trampling had unveiled it. Boyd tore it off and opened the flap.

Inside was a marble-size package, wrapped in oily butcher's paper. Boyd unwrapped it. Nestled inside was a human eye, the whole eyeball. A blue-eyed orb—fresh, from the looks of it.

Boyd rewrapped it, put it back in the pouch. He started to throw it away, checked the urge.

Evidence.

Might be useful. Still, he'd be damned if he was carrying it on him. That was above and beyond the call of duty.

If he didn't carry it, who would? Couldn't risk losing it . . .

Wincing, he tucked it into a vest pocket.

"Damnation," he said, without heat.

What else might Scarecrow have hidden on him? If Boyd missed it now, it might be lost during the descent, lost forever. A vital clue, perhaps.

Boyd gave Scarecrow a pat-down search, feeling

the folds of his buckskins for secret pockets, hidden caches. He found a few concealed weapons but no clues, vital or otherwise.

Using his knife, he cut off the legs of the dead man's breeches below the knees, slicing them into strips. He loaded the corpse on its back on the travois, using the rawhide strips to bind it to the wooden framework.

Scarecrow's rifle was a good one: Winchester, recent model, well cared for. It was evidence, too. Boyd unloaded it, then secured it to the corpse litter.

Wind brought tears to his eyes. He blinked them away. Damn, it was cold!

The cloud covered the northern half of the sky. Its leading edge bristled with little wispy curls, writhing snakelike, straining for the zenith.

In the southern half of the sky dome, the sun was shining.

In the east was a daylight moon, a pale, smudged disk.

Boyd had a feeling he was being watched. He kept on doing what he was doing, not tipping his hand. Without seeming to, he looked around. He was good at looking at things while seeming to be looking somewhere else, a useful skill in his line of work.

He saw no one, nothing out of the ordinary. But the feeling remained.

He'd left a number of clipped branches protruding from the bottoms of the posts, which were now joined to form the apex of the travois. The short-horned pegs served as convenient handholds. He gripped one in his left hand, lifting the front of the travois.

In his right hand was the carbine, ready if he needed it.

He dug his feet into the ground and pulled at the travois. It didn't budge. The job would have been easier with two hands, but he didn't want to let go of the carbine. It had a comforting feel.

He leaned forward, putting his weight into it. The travois broke free of the earth's grip, inching forward, burdened by Scarecrow's dead weight. The poles served as runners, easing the progress of the load.

Boyd slogged onward, to the lip of the cleft. He leaned forward, upper body tilted at almost a forty-five-degree angle. He let his weight pull the travois. It was slow going.

Descending into the cleft was tricky. He found a place where the lip was worn away, lessening the drop-off. He stepped down, drawing the sledge after him.

It down-tilted, sliding into the cut. Boyd braked it by lowering its nose.

In the cut there was no wind. Its absence was a blessed relief, bringing home to Boyd just how cold it had been.

He wedged the travois against a tree, immobilizing it. Then he went to the top of the cleft, rifle in hand. He lay prone, peering through golden dried weeds at the plateau park.

It was empty, lifeless. What movement there was, was inanimate—streaming clouds and wind whipping the surface of the lake, whose waters had turned leaden when the sunlight fled. The woods ringing the park were dark, oppressive.

Boyd narrowed his eyes, protecting them from windborne chaff. He watched, waited.

Straggling birds darted into the trees, seeking shelter. Some were overpowered by the wind, swept away into the rushing heights.

Boyd withdrew. The sledge left a trail as plain as railroad tracks. Snowfall would cover it eventually, but not for a while. Until then, it could be followed.

Boyd would be ready for the followers, if any. He hoped they would come. That would save him the necessity of a return trip.

He took hold of the sledge and resumed his downward trek. Wind shook the treetops, causing the trunks to sway, creaking. At ground level, where he was, the air was still.

He followed the contours of the cut, seeking the easiest path, which was rarely the straightest. Wide detours were necessary to navigate the sledge through the timber.

Getting downhill was slow going. The travois helped. It was better than dragging the corpse at the end of a rope.

The bottom of the cleft played out into a fan of loose dirt and stones spilling onto the ledge. Nearby lay the girl, She was white, bloodless, the color of dirty snow.

Boyd stood in the open, under the sky. The northern half of the dome was all stormclouds; the southern half was clear, sun shining. The dark half seemed to suck the light out of the clear part. Blue skies dulled, turning glassy.

Snowflakes began to fall. The cliff blocked most of the wind, but Boyd was still cold. He went to the horses. He put on his jacket, gloves. He flexed his hands. Soon they were warm and supple.

The horses were skittish. Blindfolded, they smelled death. Boyd soothed the gray with gentle words and hands. The packhorse was too stupid to stay scared for long.

Boyd wrapped the bodies in blankets. He tied the girl across the gray and Scarecrow across the packhorse, making the animals unhappy. He transferred the packet containing the eyeball to a saddlebag on the packhorse.

He went first. One hand held the carbine, the other held the lead rope. The horses trailed behind, first the gray, then the other.

Boyd went west, retracing his route along the cliffside trail. The trail angled downward. The place of the cleft vanished behind a curve of the rock. There was another curve, and another.

The gorge was vast, titanic. Man and horses were three specks of motion crawling down the string of the trail. The clifftop was hundreds of feet above; the valley, hundreds of feet below.

Now the sky was all gray, what Boyd could see of it, a wide band framed by the canyon walls. It was snowing hard. Big fat wet flakes pelted Boyd. Beads of melted snow clung to the underside of his hat brim. As they fell, they were replaced by others.

Snow clung to the trail, making it still more slippery. The air was heavy. Rain fell, mixed with the snow. Chill winds gusted. Boyd could see his breath. Something stung the back of his neck. Ice! The rain had turned to tiny ice particles. They drummed against the top of his hat. Winds blew harder, bombarding him with icy needles.

The largest particle was no bigger than a grain of rice. Handfuls of them fell hissing to the ground.

The horses were balky, but at least the sleet distracted them from their grisly burdens. Boyd halted under a rock overhang that sheltered this part of the trail from the storm.

The sleet spent itself, growing finer until it merged with the falling snow. The temperature had dropped below freezing. Melted snow on Boyd's hat had hardened to a thin icy crust.

He moved on. The animals were easier now that the sleet had stopped. Dark gray skies shed masses of snow, with no sign of a letup. Flakes were sharp, hard-edged, crystalline. They sprinkled the earth, dusting it with powder. White grew, blotting out greens and browns.

The twisty canyon broke the gale's main force, but stray winds whipped around corners, moaning low. A lonesome sound.

Boyd was about two-thirds of the way down the trail. Patches of wildflowers stuck their heads out of the snow.

The snowfall absorbed sound, muffling it, laying down a hush.

Dust fell, brown against the snowflakes. Boyd looked up.

A piece of the clifftop came hurtling down. It grew, filling the sky. Boyd jumped back, tripped, and fell.

A rock weighing several hundred pounds hit the ledge, striking a dozen feet further down the trail than Boyd was. He lay on his back, still holding the lead rope and the carbine. He kept the carbine muzzle up.

Two figures lurked at the edge of the clifftop, their ragged outlines blurred by the storm. Their posture was menacing, hostile. Savage. Scarecrow had possessed a similar aura.

One of the two, though not large, was very much larger than the other. A woman and child? Wild woman and devil child! No, not a child—there was something dwarfish about its proportions—

Whoever they were, they were trying to kill him. Boyd, one-handed, was pointing the carbine at them when the boulder struck.

The impact burst like a cannon shell, hammering the earth. The missile took a bite out of the ledge.

Rocks clattered all the way down to the bottom of the cliff.

The horses reared, straining at the lead rope. Boyd held it in his left hand, hitched around his elbow for support. The gray danced on its hind legs, dragging Boyd backward.

A grapefruit-size rock struck close, splashing him with mud.

The attackers were already out of sight.

Boyd got his feet under him. His attention was split

between the rock throwers and the horses. The horses were frantic. Boyd was in danger of being trampled or dragged over the side. The gray was near the edge. Working the rope, Boyd guided it toward the cliff.

Motion flickered above. Boyd fired. The bullet struck the clifftop, splintering rock.

A gratifying howl of pain followed.

The shot sent the horses into new paroxysms. It was no small matter getting them under control.

A rock fell, missing the ledge entirely.

Afraid to show themselves, Boyd thought. Maybe the worst was over.

From above came a dull pounding, as much felt as heard. A *thwacking,* as of a mallet being repeatedly hammered home.

Next came a sharp *crack!* Stones and dirt jetted from the base of jutting rock at the clifftop.

Holding the gray's bridle, Boyd hurried the animal down the trail, jogging alongside it. He was on its left, with his back to the drop.

The pounding continued. No targets for the carbine.

The gray crowded Boyd to the edge. He had to step lively to keep from falling off at the new gap in the ledge.

He kept turning the horse's head, leading it toward the cliff. The animal was moving fast now, faster than Boyd liked, making him fight to curb it. Boyd's feet flew under him. A misstep would be fatal.

The packhorse balked, slowing the gray, allowing Boyd to get it under control. Boyd panted, his legs trembling.

The pounding went on uninterrupted. The hammerer was a demon for work. Another sharp *crack!*

A shower of dirt, then a rockfall. The rocks were all of a type—smooth, round riverbed stones. They sprayed from a pair of notches at both sides of the spur thrusting out from the clifftop.

A moment before, the notches hadn't been there. Now, they grew with each passing second, opening great tears in the earth, separating the spur from the rest of the rim.

Riverstones poured out of the notches at both ends. There must be a bed of them, in a trench dug at the base of the spur. The faster they flowed, the faster the rock sagged.

Boyd urged the gray forward. The packhorse lagged, hanging back.

Boyd leveled the carbine at the horse's head, ready to shoot, cut the rope, and away.

"Move," he said.

Something in his tone convinced the blindfolded horse to start forward.

A last few stones dribbled from the vents. Borne down by its own weight, the rock spur nodded.

Twenty-five yards down the trail stood a tree. Boyd made for it, horses in tow. He went fast, but not too fast. If he went too fast, the horses would break into a run. Too slow, and the spur would get him.

Blanket-wrapped bodies jiggled but stayed tied in place. Behind, the spur was coming unhinged from the cliff.

Ahead was the tree, growing out of the cliffside at

a forty-five-degree angle. Stunted, no bigger than a man, its stem was twisted from following the sun in the depths of the gorge.

Boyd threw some hitches of rope around the base of the trunk, which was little thicker than his ankle. He stood with his back to the cliff, legs braced, holding the rope in both hands.

The spur parted from the clifftop, sliding down the rock face with a locomotive's rumble. With it came a line of poles, pilings that had been driven deep into the earth at the base of the spur. Chains held them together.

Big as a house, the juggernaut skidded off the ledge below, wiping it clean.

It struck bottom like a cannonade.

Boyd strained at the rope, fighting spooked horses. Without the tree as a bracer, he would have lost the fight. As it was, it was touch and go there for a while, especially when the tree threatened to tear loose from its roots.

Up from the valley flew a cloud of dust.

The landscape shook. Thundering echoes rippled outward from the crash site.

The horses kicked and stamped. To his alarm, Boyd found his end of the rope slipping out from between his gloved hands. He tightened his grip, arresting the slide. He had strong hands, but it was an effort to maintain his grip.

Tremors stilled, echoes faded. Boyd's grip, the rope, and the stunted tree outlasted the horses' frenzy. The spasm passed, leaving the animals shaken but

unhurt. Blind chance had kept them from falling off
the edge.

Boyd could guess how the trap had been rigged.
Sharpened stakes, as big as roof poles, had been
driven into the earth in a line where the rocky spur
jutted out from the clifftop, making a wedge in the
base. The chains on the pilings perhaps helped to an-
chor the weight, linking it to a trigger mechanism.
The trap was sprung by knocking out a linchpin, ex-
plaining the hammering that preceded the attack.
Chocks were struck off, freeing the fall of the cached
river stones, activating a counterweight. The counterweight finished the job that the stakes had begun,
shearing off the spur.

This was no casual defense. Its makers had gone
to considerable time and effort to build the trap. This
was their territory and they wouldn't quit it without
a fight.

Who were they?

The clifftoppers were nowhere in view. They were
near, no doubt, lurking under cover. They and Scarecrow must be part of the same outfit, but what that
outfit was, was a mystery.

Two

Boyd made camp at the foot of the Blue Pine Hills, in a clearing that was part of a broad, flat bench skirting the southern slopes. On all sides, pine forests screened out most of the landscape. Somewhere miles to the north lay the fatal canyon. Boyd had descended the cliffside trail without further incident. Other traps might have been hidden along the route, but if they were, they remained unsprung. Boyd saw no trip wires, no snares, but then he hadn't seen anything wrong with the spur until it parted from the cliff.

Many times he looked for the savage duo, but he never saw them. When he reached the canyon floor, he checked the corpses, securing the rigging where it had worked loose from the horses. He removed the blindfolds from the horses' eyes. Sighted and on flat land, they were still skittish. Boyd gentled them, firmly and briskly, not wanting to spend overmuch time in the gorge. The clifftops were veiled by the snowstorm. Sundown was hours away, but the storm had brought premature dusk. Boyd mounted up, sharing the gray with the dead girl. He rode out, the packhorse trailing. Canyon walls opened, shrinking as they did so. A stream trickled down the middle of the canyon floor, inky-black against the snow. The gorge opened on a shallow bowl-shaped valley. The stream splashed down a slope, snaked across a flat, and butted against the base of the opposite ridge. It turned left, following the ridge east for a few hundred yards before vanishing into a thicket.

The thicket cloaked a gap in the ridge. The stream ran down a narrow gulley. The banks were high, smooth, and rounded. A trail wound lazily down one of the banks. Boyd took it. The woods were so close to the trail that branches brushed his shoulder. Tall trees thrust skyward, making a canopy of their boughs. They blocked some of the snow and much of the light. The little daylight that was left was fading fast. The trail led into a glen, dark and still. Tree trunks stood out against the gloom like pillars in some vast, dim palace. The trees swayed, groaning, as storm winds buffeted their tops.

At ground level, it was so calm that a candle flame would have burned upright, not flickering.

The stream and the trail diverged. For a time, Boyd could hear the stream but not see it. The liquid gurgle faded, lost in the forest arcades. The trail followed the path of least resistance down through a series of wooded hillsides that fell away to the south like terraces. The storm blew harder.

From a clearing, Boyd looked down on a great

broad band of treetops, stretching out in a sweeping, crescent-shaped arc. This was the bench, a flat-topped rock formation skirting the southern slopes of the Blue Pines. The skirt was wooded. Scattered through the forest were open groves and glades. The storm was raw and stinging at Boyd's vantage point. He rode down, into the woods.

The bench was no more than a few miles across at its widest. South of the rim, the land fell away into countless hillocks and gullies. Boyd would not care to try to find his way through there at night, and day was nearly done. No, he must camp here, on the bench. In the woods.

He knew the place he wanted, one he'd passed on the way up. An open glade, circular, a hundred yards in diameter. At its center rose a bald-topped rock knob, as big as a town church. Its sides were smooth, sheer. Boyd pitched camp under the knob's south face, sheltered from the brunt of the storm. The horses were tended: unsaddled, rubbed down, groomed, watered, fed, and secured for the night in a makeshift corral consisting of several lengths of rope and some trees. They were hobbled, too.

Boyd built a fire under a slanted, overhanging slab at the base of the knob. There was plenty of dead wood. The clearing was in the deepest part of the woods. Its stony ground was part of a single formation that had given birth to the knob. It was barren compared to the dense forest ringing it. The trees all leaned inward, tilting forward to catch the life-giving sun that must stream into the open glade. Trunks were long gray ribs curving upward to a dark disk of sky. Writhing clouds shed snow.

Dead trees abounded. Some lay on the ground. Others, whose fall had been arrested by their neighbors, stood slanting at crazy angles. Many dead trees were strewn about the glade. Spiky with broken branches, overgrown with thick brush, they resembled barricades of some long-forgotten outpost.

Boyd made ready for night, which was falling fast. In the lee of the knob, protected from the winds, he built a fire. The titan rock served as a firescreen, catching the heat and throwing it back. Nearby stood a mound of firewood, more than enough to last the night.

Boyd took off his boots, noting with approval that his feet were dry. He pulled on an extra pair of socks, thick woolen ones. He put his boots back on. In this weather, it was vital to keep the feet warm and dry.

He did some things to secure the site. Then he ate. He wolfed down a quick meal of dried beef and stale biscuits, washing it down with water. He ate outside the firelight, in the shadows, hunkered down with his back to the rocks.

The horses were penned to one side of the fire; opposite them, on the other side, lay the corpses. Far from the heat, two blanket-wrapped bundles lay side by side on a snowbank. Horses and bodies both were in the firelight, where Boyd could see them.

He threw fresh fuel on the fire. Clouds of orange embers leaped up to meet falling snowflakes. Boyd laid out a bed of pine boughs near the campfire. He

used plenty of pine boughs. Blankets served to make
up his bunk, which lay on the far side of a shallow
natural basin at the foot of the knob.

Snow fell hard until about ten o'clock that night.
An hour later, the clouds had shaken out their last
few flakes and the wind had died down.

The fire burned low, a sleepy smoky-orange glow.
A shudder of unease went through the horses.

The woods were never silent, not at night. Branches
scraped, rattled, creaked. The wind, surely, and the
trees settling. Nothing more.

At half past eleven, things started popping.

Boyd had made his bunk but did not sleep in it.
He lay hidden in a hunter's blind a good stone's throw
from the campfire, behind a fallen log. After rigging
his blankets up in a none-too-convincing likeness of
a sleeping man, he'd low-crawled to a covert he'd
chosen earlier. It was to the west of the knob, on the
same side of the horses but farther out, and on a slight
elevation. A tangle of thornbushes massed on the
knoll, seemingly impenetrable. Boyd crawled under
them, then over a downed tree. On the other side was
a niche, an open space in the heart of the thicket.
Boyd had discovered it earlier while collecting firewood. He'd prepared it for later, for the vigil to come.

Boyd occupied the nest. Plenty of room to crawl
around on his hands and knees, so long as he didn't
try to stand up. The densely interlaced bushes kept
out most of the snow. He did what he could to make
himself comfortable. This was his post, he would be
here for quite some time. A folded blanket lay be-

tween him and the ground. It would help keep his limbs from stiffening from the immobility and the cold.

He missed the fire's cheery glow. The temperature hovered somewhere around the freezing point. Cold, but not killing cold. And why not? After all, it was early May. Nothing freakish about a May snowstorm in the Montana mountains, not when it was coming after the bitterest winter in living memory.

Boyd got his mind right with his surroundings. He neither watched, listened, nor waited. He just *was*.

The storm left behind a foot and a half of snow. The landscape was white, calm, pristine.

Firelight dimmed to a sullen red glow. Soon after, the horses became restless.

Hair rose on the back of Boyd's neck. The rest of him was motionless as before.

After a time, the horses settled, though they were still uneasy.

That meant that the intruders had moved away from the horses, but were still nearby.

Shadows flickered at the edge of the light.

Boyd's weapons were at hand. So was the knotted end of a piece of rope. The rope stretched back to the campsite and was buried under snow. Boyd pulled the rope.

One of the corpses moved, shuddering on a snow-bank.

Gunfire—a six-gun. Muzzle flashes speared the darkness, blazing from a point between the campfire and the corpses.

A shooter had popped up, seemingly from nowhere, and started blasting. The dark, ragged figure crouched, holding the gun in both hands, pumping slugs into the body that had moved.

A buffalo gun is .50 caliber. Boyd's octagonal-barreled six-foot-long rifle was a big .70.

He fired. A thunderbolt crashed, striking down the intruder.

From another part of the clearing came two more blasts. In the corner of his eye, Boyd glimpsed the movement and threw himself facedown a split second before the shots.

A double load of shotgun pellets ripped the covert. Boyd was safe behind a fallen log, which quivered under the barrage. Handfuls of severed brush rained down.

It all happened in the space of a few heartbeats, shots popping like a string of firecrackers.

Boyd came up with the carbine, searching for a target. As the muzzle rose, the second intruder broke cover.

In an eyeblink, he—*it*—was gone.

Boyd recognized the smaller of the two lethal cliff-toppers. No child, he. From the waist up, he was husky, powerful, with oversized arms, shoulders, and chest. Below was stunted, dwarfish, with squat, bandy legs. He was four feet high, shaggy-haired, with the face of a fiend. He vaulted a rock one-handed and disappeared.

Boyd did not rush in pursuit. Sudden moves could be fatal.

The fire dwindled to a heap of ashes with a cool, pale-yellow glow at its heart.

From the depths of the forest came a distant cry, high-pitched and wailing, mournful.

The horses pawed and stamped.

The cry was not repeated.

For the rest of the night, Boyd made no fire, nor did he sleep. Neither did he follow the dwarf's tracks in the snow.

Of course, the dead intruder was the dwarf's partner, the wild woman. Boyd got a good look at her at first light.

Wild woman indeed! A wizened, rail-thin, hating hag in dirty buckskins and moccasins. Bird's-nest hair, possum teeth, sallow skin, clawlike yellow nails. She wore a gunbelt, with extra holes punched in the strap to buckle it tight enough to keep from falling off her skinny hips.

The gun was in her hand. She'd shot well enough, dropping a tight cluster of slugs into the middle of a blanketed corpse.

Boyd had known that the dummy "sleeper" he'd arranged at the campfire would not fool the stalkers. In fact, he'd counted on it. Surreptitiously he'd tied a rope to Scarecrow's ankles, playing the line out across the ground, hidden in the snow, stretching to his sniper's nest. When the skulkers made their move, Boyd pulled the rope. Sudden movement from an unexpected source drew gunfire. Boyd fired at the shooter, tagging her in the middle. It looked like she'd been struck with a pickax.

Too bad the dwarf had gotten away. Boyd would have liked to go after him. No doubt the dwarf would have liked it, too—having the stranger come after him in the dark on his own home ground, where unknown, unguessed traps awaited.

Boyd gobbled a cold, comfortless breakfast. The sky lightened. He was ready to move. He mounted the gray. The packhorse was laden with Scarecrow and Scarecrow's victim.

The wild woman was left behind. Boyd had all the bodies he needed. For now, anyhow.

That .70 slug had made a real mess. Boyd tied a rope to the wild woman's ankles and hung her upside down from a tree limb. Dead weight swung like a pendulum, creaking the rope.

A raven fluttered to a landing on the branch near the taut rope, a big black bird with glittering eyes and a cruel beak.

Boyd rode out, looking back when he reached the edge of the clearing.

The raven clung by its talons to the woman's inverted head, pecking an eyeball. It paused to croak a warning at another of its kind, which had just alighted on the branch above.

Three

At the edge of the forest, Boyd heard a cry. It sounded again, high-pitched, piping.

Boyd rode south, out of the Blue Pine foothills. Before him lay a flat tableland, part of a wide prairie. High prairie, seven thousand feet high. The storm had spent most of its force on the upper slopes. The plain was snow-covered, but only to a depth of a few inches.

The woods thinned, replaced by masses of light and space. Trees seemed ghostly, insubstantial, as Boyd broke out into the open. Thin gray clouds hid the midday sun. In some places they came undone, baring patches of cool blue sky. Wind rustled dried bronze weeds, where they stuck up out of the snow. The temperature was above freezing. The air was wet, heavy.

Looking south: in the near ground, Ambush Meadow; in the middle ground, a curving set of railroad tracks, complete with train; and, in the far ground, a handful of pyramids that were mountains.

The train idled, smoke puffing from the stack. A steam whistle hooted, announcing itself as the source of the shrill piping cries.

Boyd rode the gray, the packhorse trailing. He made for the train. He had not gone far from the forest when he heard a cry. Not the whistle, another cry.

The cry of the dwarf.

Boyd looked back. The woods were dark, impenetrable, rising up and up to the north.

If the dwarf could have done something, he would have. The cry was his rage at being cheated of Boyd.

Boyd turned his face to the south, to the train. Still, his back felt exposed, vulnerable.

Antlike blurs moved around the train, resolving themselves into men. The train consisted of an engine, tender, baggage car, private car, livestock car, caboose. Rails gleamed dully in the wan light.

The train stopped its whistling. In the silence, Boyd could hear the engine's muffled *chuff-chuff-chuff*ing. Two pale oval faces hung framed in the square side window of the cab, watching his approach. A man with a rifle stood silhouetted on top of the slatted stock car. Another stood on the ground. Both held their weapons at port arms, not pointing them at the stranger. Yet.

Boyd rode in, coming easy, hands always out in the open. He was recognized by a sentinel, who gave the all-clear to the others. Tension lightened, but not too light, not with Boyd bringing in two bodies.

Wendell Carr, the train guard, was stocky, oxlike,

with bored brown eyes in a stolid, lumpy face. He lifted a hand in greeting, or at least recognition. Boyd nodded.

Carr said, "What you got there, Boyd?"

"Dead folks."

Boyd reined in, stepped down. Stiff and sore, he stretched his legs.

In the locomotive cab were engineer O. P. Stubbs and fireman George Krater. Grouped on the ground near the tail of the train were conductor Alf Brown and the brakemen, Henshaw and Megrim. On the baggage car roof was Fred Holtz, young assistant to the group's now absent wrangler.

Boyd said, "Watch the woods, Fred."

Holtz started. "Huh? How come?"

"I killed one, but there's others." Boyd spoke loud enough to be heard at both ends of the train.

"Killed two, that is, but I left one behind," he said.

Carr grunted, a response that might have meant many things or nothing. "You got two."

"The other's some poor gal who was trying to get away. He killed her, and I killed him," Boyd said.

Carr's dull eyes flickered with interest. "This what we been looking for, Boyd?"

"If it's not, it should be. This's a low-down dirty bunch."

"Well, you got one."

"Two."

Carr smirked. "You can't collect no bounty on a body that ain't there."

Boyd looked at him. His face didn't change. One

instant he was looking elsewhere, the next he was looking at Carr. That was all. Under that look, Carr's smirk dissolved, his face stiffening.

He said quickly, "I don't doubt you, Boyd. I'm just saying that Skinflint Dunne won't pay off without a body, that's all!"

Boyd tilted his head, as if allowing that Carr's statement might be true.

"There'll be bounties aplenty before this is done," Boyd said.

Holtz, edging the stock car roof, cleared his throat. "How many of 'em you say there was, Boyd?"

"I don't know. There's two less of them, though. One was a fair rifle shot," he added.

Carr said, "You make a nice fat target up there, Holtzie!"

Holtz crouched, shoulders hunched, eyes squinting toward the woods.

Brown, the conductor, who'd been standing within earshot, now joined the scene. He had white hair, a clean-shaven red face, and dark blue eyes.

Stifling a shudder at the sight of the corpses, he said, "More dead ones! They don't call this place Ambush Meadow for nothing!"

Boyd turned his cool-eyed gaze on the conductor. "Why do they call it that, Mr. Brown?"

Brown looked away from the dead, lifting his eyes north to the wooded hills.

He said, "Goes back forty, fifty years. Trappers'd come down from the hills, loaded with furs. Robbers'd wait for them here, where the trail ends, to kill them and steal their furs.''

Carr said, ''That was a long time ago, old-timer.''

''Those two on the horse look mighty fresh!''

Carr sniffed, making a face. ''They don't smell that way.''

''Hey,'' Boyd said.

When he had their attention, he said, ''Where's the rest of our bunch?''

''At Reinhardt's ranch. Some of his stock was killed.''

''Killed? How?''

''I don't know.''

''Torn up, like the others?'' Boyd pressed.

''I don't know. That's what Dunne and them went to see,'' Carr said. ''We're supposed to meet them at Packer Point.''

''Let's go,'' Boyd said.

Leading the horses, he crossed to the baggage car. Brown, short-legged, had to walk vigorously to keep up.

He said, ''I don't mind telling you, I'll be glad to be quit of this place! With all the black deeds it's seen—!''

Boyd hitched the lead rope to a metal staple on the side of the railroad car, securing the horses. He climbed up into the car and swung the sliding door wide open.

''Here, now! What're you doing?'' Brown said.

''Taking on passengers,'' Boyd said.

Brown, eyes popping, stared at the corpses. "You mean—*them*?!"

"Can't leave them here."

"But—the baggage car?!"

"Here's how I got it figured, Mr. Brown: I can't put them in the private car, or the fellows'd get mad. Can't put them in with the horses. And I don't reckon that you'll have them in the caboose—"

"Certainly not!" Brown sputtered, more red-faced than ever.

"—So, the baggage car it is," Boyd said.

Carr sidled over. "Money in the bank, huh, Boyd?"

"That's right," Boyd said pleasantly. "I sure can use it."

"Blood money," Carr said. He turned to the conductor.

"A bounty on every rustler's head, payable by the Cattleman's Protective Association. What do you think about that, Brown?"

Brown recoiled. "Don't tell me! I don't want to know!"

Carr laughed. "Hear that, Boyd? He don't want to know."

Brown said spiritedly, "Railroaders stick to railroading, and that's all! That was the deal!"

Boyd replied, "You're showing sense, Mr. Brown. Best pay no nevermind to things that don't concern you."

"I'm not even listening now," Brown said.

"Good. Carr, you're a big strong fellow. Give me

a hand getting this load on board, won't you?''

Unhappy, doubtful, Carr hesitated, shuffling his feet. He wore lace-up lumberjack boots, size 12, whose treaded soles left waffle-iron patterns in the snow.

"Afraid of dead folks, Carr?"

Boyd's tone was mild, mocking—doubly mocking for its mildness.

"Afraid? Hell, no," Carr said.

"Never doubted it," Boyd said. "Now, if you'll take hold over here, while I untie these ropes, we'll ease this old hoss's burden . . ."

Daylight shone through the open door into the railroad car. The long central aisle was clear. On either side, securely fastened, were stacked boxes and crates. Some of the stacks were covered with tarpaulins, others were not. Stenciled lettering on the sides of the crates identified their contents: weapons, ammunition, saddles, blankets, food, and much else. There was a smell of gun oil, powder, leather, tobacco smoke, whiskey fumes, and soot. In a corner was a cast-iron stove, unlit, ashes cold. Nearby was a desk and chair, both bolted down.

Boyd stowed the bodies at the opposite end of the car. They lay side by side on the floor, on their backs, tied down to prevent their moving during transit.

Light shone through a narrow horizontal slitted vent, high on the wall. Dust clouds scrolled through the beam. Boyd crouched at the head of the bodies.

Boyd unwrapped a blanket, baring a face. "Look here, Carr."

"Why?—I mean, sure, okay. Why the hell not?"

Fists balled, teeth clenched, Carr eyed the corpse.

It was the girl. Carr, not wincing, said, "Beaten to death?"

"Shot."

"She must have been beaten within an inch of her life first."

"Worse, but never mind about that now," Boyd said. "Is this one of the Rogers girls?"

"I sure hope not. Anne Rogers had yellow hair, like this one here. . . . Can't tell nothing from the face. Can't even hardly see a face, for all them bruises."

Carr shook his head. "Nope, I can't say for sure. I didn't know the gals, 'cept to see them in town with their folks a few times. . . . From what I can see of her, this one here looks like an old woman!"

"She was used up," Boyd said.

He pulled the blanket up, covering her face.

"Them gals was stolen over in Sun Dog, way to hell over on the other side of the pass, Boyd. That's a long ways from here."

"Especially if you're going by way of the hills, on foot," Boyd said.

He unveiled Scarecrow's face. Carr said, "Gawd!"

Boyd was on one knee, hand on the flap of the blanket he had just turned down. Scarecrow grimaced, his face a murderous, malignant death mask.

"Know him, Carr?"

"Hell, no! I sure wouldn't forget that face! Man, he looks so mad he could spit! Whew!"

Peering down, unsure of what he was seeing, Carr

said, "And them teeth, all pointy! A weasel, that's all, a goddam two-legged weasel!"

"Not so far off the mark at that," Boyd said.

Carr held his nose with one hand, fanning the air in front of his face with the other. "Phew! He's mighty ripe!"

"He smelled like that when he was alive."

"How come he's all black and swelled up?"

"Seventy-caliber round does that to you," Boyd said.

He covered Scarecrow's face, rose. Carr needed no further encouragement. He hurried out of the car, Boyd following.

A voice from above said, "Hey."

Boyd and Carr looked up. Holtz, now atop the baggage car, squinted toward the woods. He said, "I ain't seen nothing yet!"

"Keep looking," Carr said.

Boyd said, too mild, "By the way, Carr, that association bounty is open to anybody who can collect it."

"So?"

"Thought you'd like to know, in case you feel like trying your luck. There's at least one of them not far from here. Probably watching us right now."

Holtz, startled, almost lost his footing, boot heels clattering on the slippery roof. Arms windmilling, he caught his balance, saving himself from a fall. "*Dang!*"

Carr, uncomfortable, said, "We could be in somebody's gunsights."

"Never know when you're in the sights," Boyd agreed.

"Well, then, ain't we taking a chance, standing out here in the open?"

"That didn't bother you before, Carr."

"That was before I saw *him*!" Carr jerked a thumb at the baggage car, leaving no doubt as to which *him* he meant.

Carr's eyes were worried, his jaw stubbornly set. "He had a rifle, too!"

Boyd indicated the woods. "This one's partial to sawed-off shotguns. Sneaky little fellow." After a pause, he added, "He's a dwarf."

Carr brayed a disbelieving laugh, then bit it off. "You ain't funning."

Boyd shook his head. "No. But don't let his size fool you. He's dangerous."

Carr knotted his brow in a fierce frown, his sense of rightness offended.

Holtz reeled, as if struck by lightning. "I got an idea! Maybe the killers are *freaks escaped from a circus*!"

Carr snorted. "Of all the harebrained ideas—! Why, you damned fool, there's never been a circus in these parts!"

Holtz was crestfallen, abashed. Boyd said, "No carnivals?"

"A carnival came through here last year," Holtz said, brightening.

"But they didn't have no freak show," Carr said. "I know, I was there."

"Maybe they had the freaks hidden."

"Can't make no money that way. Carny don't need no useless eaters."

"That's why they escaped."

Carr started to reply, thought better of it. With an air of sorely tried patience, he sighed. "Got it all figured, huh, Freddy?"

Holtz started to squirm. "Just an idea, that's all."

"Fine. Suppose you tell it to Mr. High-and-Mighty Dunne, when we meet up with him later. I sure would like to see that! Let me know when you're going to tell him, so I don't miss it."

Brown finished talking with engineer Stubbs. Stubbs and the fireman busied themselves in the cab, while Brown turned and strode down the line of cars.

"Whenever you're ready," he said.

"Thanks, Mr. Brown," Boyd said. "Soon as the horses are squared away, we'll pull out."

"Fine." Brown, short legs churning, hurried down the line to confer with the brakemen.

Carr abruptly turned his moody gaze away from the hills. "You couldn't pay me to go in there."

Without another word, looking neither right nor left, he made a beeline for the private car.

"Climb down off there before you hurt yourself, Fred. Your business is on the ground, tending horses."

"Yessir, Mr. Boyd."

Holtz climbed down the iron ladder on the side of the car, handling his weapon so clumsily that Boyd found it prudent to step out of the line of fire.

Holtz touched down without incident. "What do you think, Mr. Boyd? I mean, about the freak show killers?"

"Who knows? The ones I saw belonged in a freak show. Or in a jar, in a museum. Maybe they'll get there yet. . . . Even so, I wouldn't mention it to Dunne, Fred."

Holtz hooted. "Haw! Think I'm crazy? Mr. Dunne's got no time for the likes of me. 'Sides, Mr. Abner'd kick my butt so hard my head'd spin, for talking out of turn!"

Excited, Holtz fumbled with his rifle, almost dropping it.

"That firearm's getting away from you, Fred."

Holtz flashed an aw-shucks grin. "I'm no gunman, Mr. Boyd, and I know it. I'm just helping out, taking my turn standing guard while we're shorthanded."

"It's right of you to do so, Fred, and I thank you for it. Now the horses need you. They've had a rough ride."

Holtz hesitated. Boyd said, "I'll stand watch."

"Okay, Mr. Boyd." Starting off at a run, Holtz went a few paces, stopped, and then returned, holding out the rifle. "You better take this, Mr. Boyd."

"Maybe I'd better." Boyd took the rifle. Holtz went to the horses, the gray and the packhorse. He unhitched them and started leading them away.

"A *dwarf*! Imagine that!" Holtz was happy-faced, full of wonderment. "Reckon that's a clue, huh, Mr. Boyd?"

"Um."

Holtz went off, leading the horses to the stock car. Boyd sighed. "Well, at least he's good with the horses."

Brown was in the baggage car, clutching the handle of the sliding door. He glared at Boyd but said nothing. His face reddened, swelling as he strained against the door. It slid shut with the solid *thunk!* of a gallows trap being sprung.

Presently the whistle sounded. Boyd got on board. With a lurch, a jolt, and a shudder, the train started forward.

The private car was usually reserved for high officials of the railroad. There was office space with desk and cabinets, a dining area, a sleeping compartment, and a lounge. The compartment was Dunne's, the others slept in makeshift bunks scattered throughout the car. Now the sole occupants were Carr and Boyd. They were in the rear of the car, in what had been the lounge. Bedrolls, traveling bags, and saddlebags were safely stowed in niches, corners, and under chairs. Carr stood at the stove, trying to stir heat from the ashes with a poker. Boyd sat at a window that faced the hills.

The train gathered speed, rolling east, leaving behind Ambush Meadow. Under a dull sky, the landscape was bleak. The snow was pitted and ribbed, so thin that the earth shadowed through it, making it look gray and dingy. Bare rock was dark with wetness. Forest showed black, except for a few dark green scallops trimming the edges. A wave of black-green foliage climbed the hills, sweeping up over the bench and beyond, into remote heights. Rising past the timberline was the naked gray rock of Mount Wendigo, heaped high with walls, galleries, spires. The summit was obscured by low-hanging clouds.

A packing trunk set on its side served Boyd as a low table. Spread across it was a blanket, on which were laid out Boyd's handguns, carbine, and a gun cleaning kit. The kit held oil, wire bristle brushes, cloth patches, rods.

Boyd set to work cleaning the weapons. The train's swaying motion, the rhythmic *click-clack*ing of its wheels, produced a pleasant lulling sensation. Boyd's concentration deepened, his movements swift and sure.

The tracks curved away from the hills, into the plain, unfolding vistas of flatland and open space. There were lone trees, clumps of woods, ridges and valleys. Under the snow lay thousands of acres of prime grazing land.

The road stretched south and east, the only sign of man and his works on the scene. No ranch houses, shacks, or sheds. No fence posts.

The line plunged almost due south for a few miles, then due east.

New facets of the Blue Pine Hills became visible, the southeastern slopes. Hanging from a sheer rock face was a vertical white thread, a waterfall that poured into a lake at the base of the cliff. Spillover from the lake had cut a channel into the plain, a watercourse that ran ever wider and deeper. This was the source of what would become the mighty Shatter River.

The channel snaked across the flat, joined by other streams from the hills. Fast-running water cut deep, vanishing beneath high banks. The cut became a scar, splintering the earth. The crack bent south, then east, widening into a steep-sided gorge whose walls were hundreds of feet high: Shatter River Canyon. From time to time, side canyons along the main route offered those on the train glimpses of the river, a vibrant black coil.

The southern horizon narrowed, a large gray landmass looming in the middle distance. This was Sentinel Rock, northernmost peak of a mountain range. Between it and the canyon the plain began to narrow.

The railroad car warmed up, thanks to the fire now burning in the stove. Carr stood facing it, his back to Boyd. Boyd broke down the carbine, cleaned it, reassembled it.

Sentinel Rock loomed, jutting out from the mountains, thrusting a broad shovel-shaped head north into the flat. Shatter River Canyon bowed south, rushing to meet it. This was the western approach to Hourglass Pass, where the plain was pinched to its narrowest point. From the heights, the flat resembled an hourglass laid on its side. The waist of the hourglass was still a good distance away.

Boyd put together the sections of a six-foot-long ramrod, a piece of hardware custom-made for his long rifle. The piece was so long that he had to stand up to clean the bore.

Outside, it began to rain, streaks pattering against the window. Boyd finished cleaning the rifle and put it away in a locking wooden gun case as the train pulled into Packer Point Station.

Four

Packer Point stood at the foot of the northernmost extension of Sentinel Rock. The station was a rectangular-shaped wooden building whose long sides ran east-west, parallel to the railroad tracks north of it. The central structure was squat, bulky, fortresslike, built close to the ground. Crude but solid. Its timbers were black with age, crusty, like the bottoms of fence posts that have stood long underground. The few windows were narrow, slitlike. The front door was stout, ironbound oak. The roof was high and peaked, with overhanging eaves, to resist winter storms.

Nearby, a subterranean spring supplied the site with an abundance of fresh, clear water, a necessity for the railroad. Standing beside the tracks was a wooden water tower. A siding split off from the main branch, terminating inside a long railroad shed. Scattered around the station were outbuildings, some sheds and a sagging barn. Behind rose the smooth-sided sugar-loaf bulk of Sentinel Rock.

The train halted in front of the station. Regularly scheduled trains were few on this branch of the line, with the next due a few days hence. Unscheduled trains would be warned of well in advance by telegraph, allowing the tracker train to pull into the siding to clear the way.

Boyd said, "Best forget what you saw under the blankets, Carr."

"I wish I could," Carr said. "Don't worry, I'll keep my mouth shut."

"When word gets out, there'll be a real ruckus."

"It'll blow the lid off this goddam valley," Carr said feelingly. "Christ, it's a powder keg now."

"Best lock up the baggage car, too."

"Hell," Carr said. He got his key ring and went to carry out the instruction.

Boyd exited the railroad car, stepping down to the platform. It was raining steadily. He tilted his hat to keep raindrops from running down the back of his neck.

Snow dissolved, baring patches of earth, giving the landscape a mangy appearance. Where grass showed, it was green, dark, and oily.

Boyd went into the station, ducking his head to avoid the low door frame. The walls were a foot thick. Inside, it was dim and musty. The floorboards were warped, buckling. A short passage led to the main hall, meeting it at right angles. This central aisle ran the length of the building. Opposite the entrance was the commons room; to the right and left were hall branchings, their walls lined with closed doors.

The commons room was barnlike, high-ceilinged. Dominating the far wall was a mammoth stone hearth and chimney. The hearth was big enough to roast an ox in, dwarfing the meager fire that now flickered fitfully in its depths. On both sides of the pillarlike chimney were long horizontal windows, their sills about five feet above the floor. They admitted the murky light of a rainy late afternoon.

On the left side of the room were some tables and chairs; on the right, a long wooden bar ran parallel to the wall. Under the left rear window, in its milky light, a lone man sat at a table, with his back to the wall. He was heavyset, with graying hair and mustache and a cold, fleshy face. He wore a dark suit, white shirt, and gun.

He played solitaire, laying down each card with a soft, scuffing snap. On the table was a whiskey bottle and a glass. He looked up, his eyes protuberant, heavy-lidded, watery. Nose and cheeks were shot through with blue-red veins.

He said, "Snow in May! Ain't this a hell of a place!"

"Um," Boyd said.

The cardplayer went back to his cards.

In the wall behind the bar, a connecting door swung open. A young woman entered the room. She was Mora Tanner, whose family owned the station. She was sixteen, slim, high-breasted. Long, straight, reddish-gold hair framed her fine-featured face. She wore a blue-and-white plaid dress and a pair of flat-heeled lace-up ankle boots.

She was calm, serious, poised. "Hello, Mr. Mc-Masters."

He touched his hat. "Miss Mora."

"Will you be staying overnight?"

"I don't know. Any telegrams for me?"

"That's Uncle Ned's job. You'll have to ask him."

"Whereabouts might he be, Miss Mora?"

"Here I am, McMasters," a voice said.

Its owner entered the big room from the center hall. Ned Tanner was middle-aged, with a lionlike head on a bearish body. Long silver-black hair covered his ears and collar. His face was clean-shaven, but he had thick, curling sideburns. A pair of round wire-rim glasses perched on his nose, lenses dulling the keenness of his gaze. He wore a green checked coat, fancy gold-and-green brocade vest, white shirt, and brown pants tucked into the tops of brown leather riding boots. He wore his gunbelt low, below his paunch.

Tanner's face split into a toothy grin. "So you made it back, eh, McMasters? I wasn't so sure I'd ever see you again!"

Mora frowned. "That's nothing to joke about, Uncle Ned—"

"He can take a joke. Right, McMasters?"

Boyd shrugged, which Tanner took to mean assent. He said, "You see, Mora, he knows that joshing is just my way of saying I'm damned glad to see him with a whole skin!"

"Of course. We all are," Mora murmured, her eyes modestly downcast.

Tanner leaned forward intently. "Tell me, what did

you find in the hills, McMasters?''

"Snow."

"Ha, ha," Tanner said, unamused. "What I mean is, did you have—*luck*?"

Kate Tanner entered, walking boldly, a big, strong, vital woman, slightly past her prime but still brimming with life force. She was five feet nine, handsome in a blowsy way, with long, curly, brick-red hair. Her face was shaped like the blade of a digging spade turned point down. Dark brows arched, flaring over a Roman nose with pinched nostrils. Moist red lips, turned down at the corners. Broad-shouldered, heavy-breasted, wide-hipped. She wore a dark rust-colored dress with a four-inch-wide leather belt. The belt worked as a waist cincher. The skirt flared out from her hips like a bell. Sewn on in the front were two deep pockets. The right-hand pocket bulged with the outline of a gun.

Her eyes glittering in a red, flushed face, she said, "Plenty of work to do in the kitchen, Mora. Our guests will be hungry tonight."

"Yes, Kate," Mora said. She went through the swinging door, into the kitchen, vanishing as the door swung shut behind her.

Kate turned on Ned Tanner, her face dark. "Don't you have sense enough not to gossip front of her?" she said. Her voice was low, intense.

"Aw, hell, Kate, she knows what's going on. Everybody in the valley knows."

"That doesn't mean you have to make it worse by

talking about it where Mora can hear. She's sensitive, high-strung.''

''Who wouldn't be high-strung, stuck out here in the middle of nowhere with a pack of kill-crazy outlaws roaming the range, killing and burning and worse?''

A whining tone had crept into Tanner's voice. He held out a hand, palm-downward. ''Shaking like a leaf . . .''

The woman sneered. ''A few drinks'll fix that.''

Tanner shook his head, *tsk-tsk*ing. ''You're a hard woman, Kate.''

''I am where Mora's concerned. I swore I'd take good care of my baby sister always, and I will!''

Tanner looked troubled. ''She's no baby, Kate. Lots of gals her age are already married with a couple of young 'uns.''

Kate's upper lip curled, baring strong white teeth. ''Fine lot of beaus for her in Shatter Valley! Drifters, cowboys, and penniless ranchers! Those the winter didn't kill or drive out have all they can do to keep themselves alive.

''And these awful murders—What the cold didn't finish, they will! If they're not stopped soon, this valley'll be a wasteland.''

Kate paused for breath, her heavy bosom swelling. In the sudden silence, Boyd heard the soft *slap!* of cards being laid out on the rear table by the stranger.

Tanner made placating gestures at the woman, as if to say, *Let it pass, let it pass.* Eyes shrewd, he said,

"Maybe Mr. McMasters has some news for us, Kate."

That took her focus off him and put it on Boyd. All the while they'd been bickering, he'd stood there motionless, waiting.

Kate said tartly, "Mr. McMasters might not appreciate your prying into his affairs, cousin."

But avid with interest, she leaned toward Boyd, as did Tanner.

Across the room, the cardplayer played on, oblivious—or so it seemed.

Boyd said, "I brought two bodies down from the mountain."

"Ah!" Tanner said. Kate gestured impatiently, shushing him.

He was not so easily silenced. His voice low, excited, he asked, "Who was it, McMasters?"

"A girl, and the man who killed her."

Kate gasped, a sudden intake of breath. "A girl! Oh, her poor mother!" She turned on Tanner. "Mora mustn't know."

"She's sure to find out. But never mind about that now. Go on, McMasters."

"That's about all there is to tell, Mr. Tanner."

"What about the killer? Who was he?"

"I don't know."

"Is he a cowboy?"

"I couldn't say. And I don't think Mr. Dunne would appreciate me making any guesses," Boyd said.

"Dunne!" Kate said.

"You know how he is."

"Humph!"

Tanner said cautiously, "He's a take-charge fellow, that's for sure."

"He's an arrogant son of a—"

Tanner cut her off. "He pays promptly, Kate. *In gold.*"

"Well, I guess he's not all bad," she said.

Boyd said, "I'd like to send a telegram, Mr. Tanner."

"Right this way, son, right this way." Tanner went into the hall, walking briskly.

Boyd, pausing, said, "The others are getting the train squared away, Miz Tanner. They'll be in directly."

She nodded. Boyd followed Ned Tanner down a branching of the hall, into the west wing. A few steps past the midpoint of the corridor, on the right side, was the telegraph office.

In the wall opposite the door, windows opened on the north, the scene dominated by the train idling in the foreground. Crewmen moved purposefully around the machine. Its bulk hid the river canyon from view, but above the top of it, mountains could be seen.

The windows were long and narrow, deepset. Below them, butting up against the wall, was the operator's desk. Secured to the desktop was the telegraph key. Emerging from terminals at its base was a pair of coiled wires, running up the wall to the corner of the window and outside.

The room was dim, musty, smelling of old paper,

wood, earth, and stone. Tanner lit a lamp. He donned
an eyeshade visor and switched on the telegraphic
apparatus, which produced a low vibratory hum.

Tanner gave Boyd some telegrams. "For you,
McMasters."

Boyd skimmed through them while waiting for the
equipment to warm up. They told him what he already
knew: Dunne and the trackers had gone on horseback
to Tingely's ranch, to investigate reports of cattle mu-
tilation. If the trail proved cold, they would return to
the station by tomorrow at the latest.

Tanner took off his bottle-green coat, hanging it
across the back of a chair. He sat down, facing the
desk, and began rolling up his sleeves.

· Boyd said, "Who's the stranger?"

Tanner looked up, brows raised, eyes narrowed.
"The gambler? Says his name's Bleekman."

"You know him?"

"Never saw him before." Tanner looked over his
shoulder, making sure the door was closed.

"Fellow's got a tinhorn look about him, Mc-
Masters. I know the type. I've been around. I haven't
spent all my days buried here at the end of the earth.
He's a gambler . . . and a bottom dealer, from the
looks of him."

"When'd he get here?"

"Night before last."

"By train?"

"No, he rode in. Alone."

Boyd's brows raised slightly. "He must be a gambler, riding alone in this country. That's betting your

life. Strange place for a gambler to light. Pickings around here are mighty slim."

Tanner said, "Maybe he had to clear out of one of those mining towns in a hurry, if you catch my drift."

"He looks too well fed for a man on the dodge. Doesn't act like one, either."

"He's a cool one."

The machine was ready to send. Boyd's message: "IMPORTANT NEW EVIDENCE STOP COME STATION NOW STOP"

One was sent to Sheriff Hutch Lattimore and another to Dr. Merritt Rhune, both in care of the telegraph office in Sun Dog town. The telegraph key cricketed as Tanner tapped out the communiqués. He had a heavy plodding touch. Oily sweat beaded his forehead as he labored.

Not waiting for the sending to be finished, Boyd said, "I'm going to get some grub."

"I'll bring you the reply soon as it's in," Tanner said, not missing a stroke in his slow, measured pounding.

Boyd went out.

Bleekman said, "Buy you a drink?"

"All right," Boyd said.

He sat down at Bleekman's table, under the rear wall window, to the left of the hearth. Bleekman kept on playing solitaire, drawing cards from the deck and rearranging the layout.

"I'm Bleekman."

"McMasters."

Intent on the cards, Bleekman leaned far forward, so that his face was almost parallel with the tabletop.

Outside, the light was failing, oppressed by low black clouds.

Mora crossed to the table where the two men sat. She now wore a white bib apron over her dress. She stood with hands primly folded in front of her.

"Your room will be ready in a few minutes, Mr. McMasters," she said.

"Thanks."

Bleekman said, "Another glass, please."

Mora turned and went to the bar, returning with a glass. She set it down in front of Boyd, straightened, looked around, frowned.

"My, it's dark," she said.

She went around the room and lit some lamps.

"Drink up," Bleekman said.

Boyd splashed some whiskey into a glass, drank it. "Ah." It burned good.

"Much obliged," he said.

Bleekman nodded. "Damnedest place, this Shatter Valley! People go around as if they're scared for their lives. Is it as bad as all that?"

"It's pretty bad," Boyd said.

"The Bloody Horrors, eh?"

"Some call it that," Boyd said.

"You hear some wild stories."

"They're some wild murders."

"Heads cut off, bodies hacked up, whole families butchered . . ." Bleekman glanced out the corner of his eye to see if Boyd would respond. Boyd sat there smiling. He smiled with his lips, no teeth showing. It was a meaningless smile.

Bleekman said, "Who's doing it? Indians?"

Boyd shook his head. "No Indians in these parts. They're long gone."

"Outlaws, then? I was warned about bandits in the valley."

"There's some holdup gangs, rustlers, and lone crooks. When the cold killed off most of the herds last winter, the ranchers had to let a lot of hands go. That put the cowboys in a tight spot, with little money and no prospects. There were bad feelings. Some of the men moved on. Others bunched up and took to the brush, living off the land. Which meant living off the ranchers, since the cold thinned out most of the wild game. The ranchers mean to hold on to the stock they've got. The cowboys don't plan to starve to death. They'll take what they need, and they're not afraid of a shooting scrape. They're rustlers mostly, but some have turned bandit. And there's always a few who'll commit any crime they think they can get away with."

"They're a damned nuisance, but they're not the ones behind the Bloody Horrors," Boyd said.

"No? Seems to me they're the most likely suspects. A handful of mean-minded types, say, out for revenge against all ranchers," Bleekman said.

"These killings were done for the love of it."

"Brrr!" Bleekman mock-shuddered. "That calls for something to warm the blood. Another drink?"

"Sure," Boyd said.

Bleekman filled both glasses to the brim. Boyd took a mouthful. Bleekman tossed his back, downing it in one gulp. This time his shudder was real. Half a minute later, red color came into his face, darkening and swelling the broken blood vessels in his cheeks and nose.

He put down his glass and resumed his cardplaying.

"There's a reward for the killers," he said—not as a question.

"A big one," Boyd said. "Plan on trying for it?"

"I'll leave that to you. Maybe you'll give me a chance to take some of it away at the card tables," Bleekman said.

"That bounty's a long way from being collected yet."

"Not too long, I hope."

"Who knows?"

Boyd saw Kate Tanner enter the central hall. He drained his glass, pushed back his chair, and stood up.

He said, "Thanks for the drinks."

"Thanks for the talk," Bleekman said.

"Next time, I'm buying."

"I'll be around," Bleekman said.

Boyd followed Kate Tanner to his room in the east wing. It was small, low-ceilinged. There was a bed, chest of drawers, night table, and chair. A wooden wardrobe closet stood against the right wall. Opposite the door, a narrow window opened high in the wall, looking south onto Sentinel Rock. The window was five feet above the floor and too narrow for a human to squirm through. The curtains were open, but the fading daylight was so weak that Kate Tanner had to light a lamp to illuminate the room.

She went out, leaving him alone. He poured water from a pitcher into a washbowl and splashed some of it on his face. His skin felt tight; his eyes, tired.

He went out of the room, not locking the door. There was nothing inside worth stealing.

At the telegraph office, a reply was waiting, a message from Sun Dog. Boyd read the telegram. Sheriff Lattimore and Dr. Rhune would meet the train tomorrow noon at Three Forks crossing.

Boyd went outside and told Alf Brown. Brown would tell the train crew.

"One more thing, Mr. Brown," Boyd said. "I'd appreciate it if the baggage car stays locked up all night."

Brown had a set of keys to every locked door on the train.

"Fine with me," Brown said. "The less I have to do with your business, the better."

The private car was unlocked, empty. Boyd went inside and got his carpetbag. There were some clean clothes in it. Uneasy, he eyed the carrying case that held the long rifle. The big .70 was unique, irreplaceable. Hefting the carpetbag in one hand, he slung the carrying case under the other arm and exited the car.

Megrim was on guard, making his rounds, walking on patrol up and down the line of the train. Boyd waved for him to come over.

Megrim was twenty-five, sun-bronzed, lantern-jawed. He wore a black hat and a long sheepskin coat. He was armed with a rifle and a holstered gun.

Boyd said, "Got your keys?"

"Sure. Carr gave 'em to me when I came on duty," Megrim said. He pulled a key ring from his coat pocket and jangled it, rattling the keys.

Boyd said, "Open the baggage car, will you?"

"Sure."

Megrim climbed the steps and stood on the platform outside the baggage car's forward door, unlocking it. The door opened. Beyond the threshold was darkness. Megrim stepped aside, clearing the path for Boyd. As Boyd moved past, Megrim smiled tightly.

He said, "When Carr came out of there earlier, he looked a mite queasy."

"Want to see?"

"Well . . . sure!"

Boyd entered the baggage car. Twilight shone through the doorway, filling the immediate area with gloom. Boyd set down the bag and the case and struck a match. A gleam flickered in the glass globe of a lamp. Boyd lit it, filling the tunnellike interior with golden light and brown shadows.

"Close the door," Boyd said.

Megrim entered, closing the door behind him, not locking it.

Boyd set the lamp down on a table. He went down the aisle to the middle of the car, a central space flanked by now-sealed side sliding doors. Hanging from the ceiling on an adjustable pull-cable was an overhead lamp. Boyd lit it. Its globe of brightness far outshone that of the hand lamp.

The bodies were in the rear of the car. There was enough light to see by. The air was close, clammy. Boyd uncovered the faces.

"Look, but don't tell," he said.

Megrim was appalled, fascinated. Boyd left him there while he went forward to secure the long rifle in a safe place.

Megrim was ready to go before Boyd was. Boyd said, "Cover the faces when you're done."

"I did," Megrim said.

Lamps were snuffed, the interior plunged back into darkness. Boyd and Megrim stood outside on the car platform while Megrim locked up.

Megrim straightened, pocketing the keys. He rattled the door to make sure it was locked.

Boyd said, "That stays locked all night."

"Right," Megrim said.

Boyd reached for a cigarillo. "Smoke?"

"Don't mind if I do," Megrim said.

Boyd handed him a cigarillo and took another for himself. He lit up, cupping the match between his hands. He drew on the cigarillo, puffing smoke.

"Takes the stink out of your nose," he said.

"What I really could use is a drink," Megrim said.

The two stood on the car platform, smoking. The roof's overhang kept the rain off them. The landscape was choked with murky darkness. The snow was almost gone, washed away. Acrid tobacco fumes mingled with the smells of rain, damp earth, and train machinery.

Megrim said, "Some face on that boy! Whew! That's a Hell Killer if ever I saw one!"

"For now, you didn't see it," Boyd said.

Megrim made a placatory gesture. "I know, I know. I wouldn't be working for the railroad if I didn't how to keep my mouth shut. Some of the stuff I've seen . . . Hell, I wouldn't be on this job if I didn't have a rep as a closemouthed man."

"Good."

"Looks like you're in for some of that reward money," Megrim said, not without envy.

"If he turns out to be one of the gang," Boyd said.

Megrim's mouth had a skeptical twist. "Yeah? What do *you* think?"

"I think he is."

"I'm sure of it. Knew it as soon as I laid eyes on him!" Megrim laughed. "That's a good one on Dunne! While he and the others are off on a wild goose chase way to hell and gone on the other side of the valley, you bag the game!"

"Maybe not a wild goose chase. This bunch we're after throws a wide loop," Boyd said.

He stubbed out what was left of the cigarillo. He picked up the carpetbag.

"Keep your eyes open," he said.

"I always do," Megrim said. Then, uneasy, he said, "You don't think they're going to try anything here, do you?"

"Why not?"

Boyd stepped down from the car and went into the station. He needed a hot meal, a bottle of whiskey, and a good night's sleep. But first he needed a bath. A coin put in the hand of Ned Tanner set the wheels in motion. He led the way, Boyd following. They went down the main corridor of the west wing, through a door on the left, into the rear of the kitchen. The kitchen was warm, steamy, filled with food smells. Kate Tanner and Mora bustled about making dinner, too busy to do more than glance at the newcomers.

The two men crossed to an archway in the opposite wall and went going through it into a passageway that passageway ran parallel to the central hall and extended along the rear of the west wing, communicating with the back rooms.

The bath house was a room added on to the rear of the structure. A lamp with a sooty globe burned smokily on a wall shelf. There was a raised wooden platform with spaces between the planks to drain run-off water. On it sat a galvanized-steel tub, partly filled. From it rose thin curls of steam.

The room was cold. Boyd could see his breath. He stuck a bare hand into the tub. The water was lukewarm.

"More water," he said. "This time, make it hot."

"You bet," Tanner said, exiting.

On a wooden shelf were folded towels, washcloths, soap, a long-handled scrub brush. Below it was a bench. Boyd unbuckled his gunbelt and unholstered his gun. He hung the belt on a hook. He sat down, placing the gun on the bench beside him.

He pulled off his boots, socks. He stripped, rolled his clothes up in a ball, and tossed it in the corner. His skin was all goose bumps and he was shivering. He stepped into the tub and sat down. It was a tight fit. His legs were bent, with the knees out of the water. The water came up to his waist. He slouched, seeking the fluid's wan warmth.

On the platform, on Boyd's right, was a wooden stool. On it lay the gun, on its side, pointing at the door.

A knock sounded on the door. "Come in," Boyd said, his hand hovering over the gun.

Holtz entered, laden with a big bucketful of hot water, whose handle he gripped in both hands.

Huffing and puffing, he lugged it to the platform and set it down. "Here go, Mr. Boyd."

"Fred? Why are you carrying water?"

"Poor Mr. Tanner's back was hurting him awful bad."

"That's what he told you, huh?"

Holtz's face fell. "Did I do something wrong? I was just trying to help out."

"You've got work enough. Stick to your chores and let Tanner stick to his."

Holtz nodded solemnly. "Yessir."

"Get some food and rest. You'll need it," Boyd said. "This game's far from done."

"Okay, Mr. Boyd."

"Now, pour that water and git!"

Later, scrubbed clean of trail grime and wearing

clean clothes, Boyd took dinner in the big room. At one table sat the train crew—Stubbs, Krater, Brown, and Henshaw. At another, Carr and Holtz. Occupying the same table and seat as earlier was Bleekman, who might well have maintained unbroken tenancy there. The cards had been put away. On the table was a new bottle of whiskey and a full dinner plate. The food was untouched, but serious inroads had been made on the whiskey.

Boyd sat alone, at a corner table. He didn't feel like talking. The meal was served by Mora, hair pinned up at the top of her head, her fine-boned face flushed red from steamy kitchen heat.

The main course was beef stew. It was watery, with lots of chopped-up potatoes, turnips, and carrots, sprinkled with a few lumps of tough, stringy meat. Biscuits helped, a serving of tinned greens didn't. For dessert, whiskey.

Carr gulped the last of his coffee and went outside. A few minutes later, in came Megrim, now off duty. He sat down at Holtz's table and ordered dinner.

Bleekman pushed his plate away, the food uneaten. From an inside breast pocket, he pulled out a packet, an envelope-size oilskin folder, bulging at the seams, its flap held shut by knotted strings. He put it down in front of him on the table. He drank a glassful of whiskey. He untied the knot, opened the folder, froze.

A shadow fell across the table. Indicating the dinner plate, Mora said, "Are you done, Mr. Bleekman?"

"Take it away," Bleekman said.

She whisked away the setting, wiped down the table, and went away.

Bleekman drained another glass. He lifted the folder flap and took out a bundle of papers. They were yellow and creased with much use. He peeled off a few sheets, unfolded them, and began studying the topmost.

After a smoke, Boyd rose and went, bottle in hand, to Bleekman's table. "Buy you a drink," he said.

"Okay," Bleekman said.

Not rushing, he gathered his papers. There were age-stained handwritten manuscript pages and old newspaper clippings. He put them in the folder and pocketed it.

"Letters from home," Bleekman said. "I'm a sentimentalist."

He blinked owlishly, indicating an empty seat. Boyd filled it. He filled Bleekman's glass and his own. They drank.

Bleekman said, "You pay for information?"

"What've you got?" Boyd said.

"Frankly, nothing yet." Bleekman leaned forward. "A man like me meets all kinds of people. No telling but what one of them'll come up with a clue."

"Any information leading to the taking dead or alive of a member of the so-called Hell Killers gang earns a share of the reward."

"How big a share?"

"The man you want to talk to is Dunne," Boyd said.

"I don't think so. Not with what I've heard about

him,'' Bleekman said. ''In the valley, wherever you go, everybody's got something to say about Dunne— all bad.''

Boyd shrugged. ''Nobody likes the top dog.''

''And Dunne is top dog around here?''

''The loudest, anyhow,'' Boyd said.

''Why can't I deal with you?''

''Go ahead. I'm listening,'' Boyd said.

Bleekman wagged a finger in front of his face, a slow, metronomic movement. ''Uh-uh. I haven't got anything yet.''

''If you get something and it's good, you'll be fairly rewarded. You have my word on that,'' Boyd said.

''Now all I need is a clue,'' Bleekman said.

Boyd rose. ''Got to make my rounds.''

''Your bottle?''

''Kill it.''

''It's most dead already, but I'll finish the job,'' Bleekman said.

''See you,'' Boyd said.

Bleekman gave a two-fingered salute.

Boyd put on a jacket and went outside. The rain had stopped. The sky was overcast. Mist banks rolled across the darkling plain.

Boyd sought out Carr, on foot patrol around the train.

''All quiet,'' Carr said.

''I'm going to take a look around before I turn in,'' Boyd said.

He crossed to the station's west wing, circling

around to the back. Behind the station was a muddy
yard. Beyond lay the corral, now empty. To the left
of the corral were some sheds. To the right of the
corral stood the barn. In it were stabled the station's
horses and the horses from the train.

Beyond the corral lay a boulder-strewn field, and
beyond that, the foot of Sentinel Rock. There was
enough cover there to hide an army.

Boyd prowled around, finding nothing suspicious.
A patch of mist brushed his face, feeling like cobwebs
against his skin. The ground was soft, wet. He went
to the barn. The horses were restless, but not unusu-
ally so.

Behind and to the right of the barn was the well
shed, a one-room wooden cabin nestled in the rocks.
A smaller well adjacent to the station supplied its water needs. The ground beneath was limestone, an extension of the formation that included Sentinel Rock.
It was porous, honeycombed with caves and underground springs. The primary spring on the site was
located back among the rocks. It was the source that
supplied the railroad water tower. It was enclosed by
a windowless structure with a peaked roof.

Boyd angled toward it, the glow of the station
lights behind him dimming with every step. The most
distant outbuilding was the well shed. Boyd approached it, gun in hand.

The well shed's long sides ran east-west. In the
wall facing Boyd, emerging from a hole in the middle
of its base, was a length of corrugated metal pipe,
about three feet in diameter. It was mounted on a

wooden frame that slanted downhill, to the water tower. Inside the shed was the spring and the pumping machinery. At its left, small side was the lone door, locked.

Boyd tried it. It remained locked. He put his ear to the door, hearing nothing from inside but liquid drippings and gurglings.

He had his night vision but not well enough to distinguish footprints in the ground. He risked a match, looking away as it flared into flame, cupping it in his hands. By its glow, he scanned the ground around the well shed. The only footprints were his own.

A lonesome place . . .

Boyd turned, taking a diagonal path to the barn. Crossing the yard, he went along the back of the station, circling the east wing to return to the train. He found Carr.

"All okay?" Carr said.

"Looks like," Boyd said. "Well, good night."

Five

Boyd woke in darkness. He was sitting up in bed, a gun in his hand.

A knock sounded on the door. Presumably that was what had wakened him. The knocking was not loud, but it was persistent.

"What?" Boyd said.

On the other side of the door, a voice said, "It's me, Tanner. It's time for your watch."

"What time is it?"

"Almost midnight."

To Boyd, it seemed as if his head had just hit the pillow an instant ago, instead of the hours that must have passed since he closed his eyes. He felt wearier than he had before sleeping.

Stifling a groan, he swung his legs off the bed and put his bare feet on the floor.

"I'm up," he said.

"You sure?" Ned Tanner said.

"Yah."

Boyd felt around the top of the night table, found a match, lit it. He lit the lamp on the table.

He heard Tanner's footsteps go away.

Boyd had slept with his pants on. He had slept with a gun in his hand. If trouble had come, he would have been ready.

He put on a shirt, socks, boots, and a gun. He rested the lamp on a cabinet that stood to the right of the door, against the wall. He opened the door. Light shone in the hall. He blew out the lamp, went into the hall, and closed the door.

He stood in the central aisle of the east wing. The room next door held Stubbs and Krater. Through the door could be heard muffled snoring. Across the hall, directly opposite Boyd's room, was the room occupied by Bleekman. No light showed from under either door. Stubbs, Krater, Boyd, and Bleekman, the only four guests to have taken overnight lodgings in the station.

Boyd followed the corridor to the main hall. The massive front door was locked and bolted. A single lamp lit the central space. At the edge of the light, the west wing corridor stretched away, a dim tunnel with a lamp shining at its midpoint.

In the big room, a table and chair stood near the low-burning hearth. On the table was a lamp, a pocket watch, an open box of shotgun shells, and a double-barreled shotgun. The shotgun lay on its side, pointed outward. The piece was broken, a safety measure.

Ned Tanner wore an oversized quilted smoking jacket, open and unbelted. Baggy pants were pulled up, waistband hiked above his belly. The tops of his long underwear showed. Bare feet were stuck into fleece-lined moccasins.

He came out from behind the bar with a bottle and a glass, which he set down on the table.

"You might get thirsty," he said.

"Thanks," Boyd said.

"Courtesy of the house," Ned Tanner said. He stifled a yawn. "Well, I'm going to get me some sleep."

"Who's up after me?"

"Krater. Your watch is from twelve to two, his is from two to four. Two-hour watches," Tanner said.

A clock stood against the wall near the end of the bar. A grandfather-type clock, in a six-foot-tall dark wood oblong cabinet. The hands on the clock face gave a time of ten minutes to three.

Ned Tanner noticed Boyd glancing at the clock. "Never mind about that. That old clock ain't worked for years. Been meaning to get it fixed, if ever there's a clockmaker in the county."

He tapped his finger on the table beside the pocket watch. "This keeps good time." He picked it up, opening it, displaying the face. The hands stood straight up. It was just about midnight.

He closed it and set it down, the watch chain links rattling softly against the table.

"That's about it," he said.

Boyd nodded. "Okay."

"There's sandwiches on a plate under the bar," Ned Tanner said.

"Fine."

"Then I'll be going."

"I'll go with you, at least partway," Boyd said. "I want a look at the train."

They crossed into the central hall.

"There's a lookout in the door," Ned Tanner said, his voice hushed so as not to disturb the stillness of the night.

A sliding panel was set in the middle of the door at eye level. Boyd opened the panel and looked out. The door was so thick that it was like looking out of a tunnel.

"Can't see much this way," Boyd said.

He wrestled with the bar across the door. It was wedged tightly into a pair of L-shaped iron hooks bolted to the door frame. Boyd hammered the underside of the bar with the heel of his palm. The bar came loose with a clatter. He lifted it from the grooves and set it aside.

He took hold of the door handle with both hands and pulled. The door was heavy, hard to move. Timbers groaned. The bottom of the door scraped against the stone floor.

"It's awful loud," Ned Tanner fretted.

"Almost done," Boyd said.

He opened the door halfway. "This place is built like a fort."

"It was a fort, seventy years ago," Ned Tanner said. "Fur traders built it to keep from being massacred by savages."

"Times sure have changed," Boyd said dryly.

Lights showed through curtained windows of the

private railroad car. Other lights showed in the caboose. The rest of the train was dark.

A figure rounded the front of the locomotive and came into view. Boyd heard him before seeing him. Trackbed gravel crunched under booted feet. Shoe leather scuffed against wooden crossties.

A man, armed with a rifle, on walking patrol. One of the train guards, Carr or Megrim, Boyd didn't know which. It was too dark to tell. The walker moved down the line, rearward along the side of the train facing the station. He walked on the ground beside the tracks.

Light from the private car revealed him as Megrim.

Boyd said, "You can go on to bed now, Mr. Tanner."

"If it's all the same to you, I'll wait till you're done. I won't sleep a wink until I've seen that door safely locked and bolted."

"I won't be but a minute," Boyd said.

He stepped outside, moving to one side of the doorway. Light from inside shone through the partly opened door, throwing a fan of yellow on the ground. Opposite it, at the train, Megrim had drawn to a stop.

Boyd called Megrim's name. He stepped into the light so Megrim could see it was him, then sidestepped into the sheltering shadows. Megrim crossed the platform to the station.

"All quiet?" Boyd said.

"Like a tomb," Megrim said, then did a double take. "Yikes! What am I saying?"

"I don't know. Is everyone squared away?"

Megrim nodded. "They're all bedded down. Carr and Holtz are in the private car. Brown and Henshaw are in the caboose."

"Funny," he said. "Half the crew sleeps on the train, and half sleeps inside!"

"Henshaw's too mean to go the price of a bed, and Brown's too much of a mother hen to leave off setting on his precious train," Boyd said.

"I'd sleep in myself, if I wasn't train guard," Megrim said. "These railroad bunks are like coffins. What I wouldn't give to stretch out on a nice soft bed—!

"I wouldn't mind stretching out on that landlady, neither," he continued, twisting his face into a leer that was more grotesque than comic.

"Maybe old Tanner can set something up," Boyd said. "He's standing on the other side of that door."

"Huh? Why didn't you tell me—? Aw, hell, we're talking low. He probably didn't hear nothing," Megrim said.

"Even if he did, he probably wouldn't use that double-barreled shotgun," Boyd said.

"Guess I'll be on my rounds," Megrim said, sidling away.

"Somebody'll be on watch inside all night. Tell Carr."

"I will," Megrim said, from a distance.

Boyd went inside. Standing in the center hall was Ned Tanner, hands stuffed in his pants pockets. If he had heard Megrim's remark, he gave no sign.

Boyd had to put his shoulder to the door to move

it. It closed with a ponderous thud. He dropped the
bar across the door and latched shut the sliding panel
of the lookout.

"I'll sleep well, knowing I'm being guarded by a
professional gun," Tanner said.

" 'night," Boyd said.

Tanner waved, shuffling down the west wing corridor. At the midpoint, below the lamp, he turned
right and opened the door to his room.

Before he could enter, the door to the room opposite his opened and Kate Tanner stuck her head out.
Her hair was unbound and fell in long brandy-colored
waves. Her profile was strong, sharp. Her bare neck
was corded, muscular. There was white lace at her
throat and the hinted curve of a white-gowned shoulder. The rest of her was hidden inside the door.

Ned Tanner turned, facing her. He went to her
door, standing outside the threshold. They spoke in
hushed voices. Boyd couldn't make out what they
were saying. Well, it was none of his business. He
moved on, into the big room.

The hearth was banked low. He put some logs on
the fire from a pile of them in the corner. Nightfall
found the station, like all other homes in the valley,
with sufficient firewood to last until dawn. Either that,
or let the fire burn itself out. Nobody was going outside in the dead of night for more fuel.

The fire blazed up. Boyd sat down, his back to the
fire. He pushed the bottle an arm's length away,
across the table from him. He wouldn't drink on
watch. He examined the shotgun. Old, but service-

able. It would get the job done. He checked the pocket watch to make sure it was fully wound.

Firelight streamers danced on the ceiling. Reflected highlights gleamed off the bottle.

Boyd, restless, got up and walked around. He drifted over to the cabinet clock. It was gnarly with elaborate decorative carvings. There were birds and beasts, flowering plants, farmers tilling a field, trees, clouds, the sun, moon, and stars. There were strange creatures, half-man, half-beast hybrids. The carvings covered the upper half of the cabinet, framing the clock face. In the lower right corner of the design, peeking out from behind a tree, was a hooded skeleton brandishing an hourglass and a scythe.

Boyd's finger traced the outline of the Reaper.

"I know you," he said.

He went to the table, sat down. He uncorked the bottle and poured a drink.

"Just one," he said.

He took a sip. No good. This stuff was too raw. He tossed it back, shuddered. Presently, warmth blossomed.

Holding up the glass, studying the light mirrored in its glittering surfaces, Boyd thought of how he had come to be here . . .

Lydia Crane was no lady. She was a beautiful young woman. Rich. She looked, dressed, and acted the part of one of the gentry. When it came to getting what she wanted, though, she was anything but ladylike.

Eighteen months earlier, Boyd had been visiting his

older brother, Warren, in Abilene, Kansas. His brother was a power in the Cattleman's Protective Association. In effect, Boyd worked for him. *With* him, actually, because they were more like partners. This was good because Boyd was a maverick type who didn't cotton to bosses. He could work with his brother, on an informal basis. No reporting to committees, going through channels, deferring to superiors. No red tape, no paper trail. The arrangement was also to the association's benefit. Some of the things that Boyd was called on to do in the line of duty were best left undocumented. The association board members were no shrinking violets, but the less they knew of the extreme measures sometimes necessary to carry out their long-range objectives, the better. What they needed to know, they trusted to the elder of the McMasters brothers to inform them. It was all done very discreetly. He spared them enough of the messy details to allow them to go on thinking that they, and he, were all a bunch of fine fellows. Boyd steered clear of them. He knew he made them uncomfortable. There was too much of the aura of the hangman about him.

On his two or three visits a year with his brother, Boyd kept away from the association offices as much as possible. His brother was proud of him and didn't give a damn who saw the two of them together. He would have quit the association on the spot if anyone had suggested that it might be more politic for him to distance himself from his semi-notorious younger brother. Boyd knew that without it having to be said, and he appreciated it. But the fact of the matter was that more than once, Boyd had gone far beyond the law to carry out his mission of protecting association members. He'd gotten away with it so far, but should the day ever come when his luck ran out, it would be better if he was not too closely identified with either the association or his brother. They both appreciated his discretion.

Which was why Boyd was surprised when his brother asked him to join him for dinner with a beautiful woman.

"If you're having dinner with a beautiful woman, what the hell do you need me for?" Boyd said.

"A fourth," his brother said. "I'm taking my lady friend. Your partner is Lydia Crane."

"Lydia Crane? Who's she?"

"She's got beauty, brains, and some mighty impressive landholdings in Montana."

"I should have known that this would involve business."

"Association business, Boyd! She's running some big herds up there. I don't mind telling you, we value her membership highly."

"So?"

"So, she's in town on a business trip, and she needs a dinner partner for tonight."

"Why don't you take her?"

"Because if I did, my current lady friend would cut my throat. And when you see Lydia Crane, you'll know why. Listen, brother, I'm doing you a favor! There's not a red-blooded male in town who wouldn't jump at the chance to be Lydia Crane's escort for the evening.''

"What about some of those buckos on the board?" Boyd said.

"They'd do it in a second—if their wives would let them. No, Boyd, this is a job for a McMasters!''

"What about Mr. Crane?"

"Deceased," his brother said smugly. "She's a widow."

"A widow woman cattle baron," Boyd mused. "Sounds tough as old saddle leather."

"She don't look it," his brother said. "What have you got to lose? I'm buying, so no matter what, you get a free feed out of the deal. And you'll be helping me out. What do you say?"

"All right," Boyd said.

"Good man. I knew I could count on you," his brother said. "Oh, and one other thing."

"Here it comes," Boyd said. "What is it? She's got two heads?"

"No. She's a mankiller."

"Um," Boyd said. "Well, at least we'll have that in common."

"Her weapons are different. And she only uses them on her husbands."

"Husbands? You mean there's more than one?

His brother held up two fingers. "Two—that we know of. Both were rich, older men, past their prime. You know the story: older man tries to keep up with a frisky young bride . . . The spirit is willing, but the flesh is weak."

"You saying what I think you're saying?"

"Let me put it this way, Boyd—both husbands died in bed. From what I heard, Lydia made their last days very, very happy. And they made her a rich widow."

"A Black Widow! Now, I see why you didn't want to risk any of those old goats on the board," Boyd said.

His brother looked mildly offended. "Hey, most of them aren't much older than I am!"

"Uh-huh."

"But you're right. We can't risk any big dues payers."

"Ain't you worried I might suffer the fate of the previous Mr. Cranes?"

"We should all be that lucky," his brother said. "You look healthy enough. Besides, you ain't rich!"

"Don't I know it," Boyd said.

His brother grinned. "If she does go for you, it'll be for the pure sport of it!"

"I'm a sporting man myself," Boyd said.

That night a foursome met for dinner in a private box at the Golden Eagle, one of the town's premier eateries. Boyd wore a gray suit, white shirt, and holstered gun. His brother, more citified, had a pocket pistol. His brother's lady was Amanda Westerfield, a banker's daughter. She was about fifteen years younger than her escort. She was pretty and well built. Sunflower-yellow hair, worn loose, framed her round, open face. Her eyes were dark blue. Her brows were thick and dark. They made her look intelligent. Her nose was slightly snubbed. Her pink-lipped mouth was mobile, expressive.

A soft blonde dressed in bright pastels, levelheaded but not stuffy.

Lydia Crane was a steel blonde. She was about Boyd's age, with the face and figure of a woman ten years younger. Tall, slender, and long-limbed. A fine-boned face, features sharp and clean, with high cheekbones. Her cheeks were slightly sunken, giving her a hungry look. Fine, ash-blond hair was piled on her head in a tight, elaborate coiffure. Wide, dark eyes. The contrast with her blondness made the eyes look twice as deep. Her skin was pearly-pink, the same color as the inside of a seashell. She wore a form-fitting black jacket, frilly white blouse, ankle-length black skirt, and pointy-toed black shoes.

Boyd's brother handled the introductions.

"Boyd's a top association troubleshooter," he said.

Lydia Crane smiled politely. "What exactly does that mean?"

"When I find trouble, I shoot it," Boyd said, not being smart, just stating a fact.

Lydia Crane's smile became less polite and more thoughtful.

"Boyd's a range detective," his brother said quickly. "He protects stockmen from rustlers, bandits, sheepherders, sodbusters, and other pests."

"Chasing stray cows? Sounds dangerous," Lydia Crane said.

Boyd nodded solemnly. "Almost as dangerous as being married."

His brother winced. Amanda's blue eyes widened. Lydia Crane looked startled, then laughed out loud.

"Married to me, you mean! Well, I guess I had that coming," she said.

Then, "You are dangerous," she said.

"Maybe we'd better declare a truce," Boyd said.

"Better still, let's drink on it," Lydia said.

They drank champagne, the ladies' choice. The Golden Eagle was a first-class dining place, in a town flush with well-heeled cattle buyers and sellers, so champagne was readily available. Once poured, the bubbly liquid in the glass was the same color as Lydia Crane's hair. The consensus was that it was pretty good champagne. Boyd didn't know. The stuff didn't give him much of a lift, but he stayed with it for a few glasses to be sociable.

Fancy-dressed waiters served the various courses, and the wine that went with them. On the white-clothed table were crystal goblets, fine china plates, glittering cutlery.

Lydia Crane and Boyd were deep in conversation. The topic: cattle. Raising, buying, selling, grazing, and improving the breed. The woman knew her stuff.

Satisfied that Boyd and Lydia Crane were getting on nicely, Boyd's brother devoted his attention to Amanda. A few glasses of wine made her eyes sparkle and put color in her face.

The evening was a success. It ended prematurely. Amanda Westerfield, a respectable unmarried young woman, was due home at a decent hour. Her parents, Mr. and Mrs. Banker, would be waiting up. Boyd's brother took her home. Her home, that is.

The hotel where Lydia Crane was staying was near the Golden Eagle, diagonally across from it on the square. Boyd took her arm, escorting her. The folds of her skirt rustled, brushing against his hip.

They climbed the columned hotel steps, entered the lobby. There was fancy wallpaper, polished wood, brass chandeliers, carpets, overstuffed furniture.

Lydia Crane said in a low voice, "Room fourteen. Come by the back stairs. My maid, Drusilla, will let you in."

Adroitly disengaging from his arm, she said in a normal tone of voice, "Thanks for a lovely evening."

"The night's young," he said.

"It's been a long day. I'm ready for bed." The way she said it, it sounded like she meant she wanted to go to sleep.

"Good night," she said.

"See you," Boyd said.

"Yes," she said.

She turned, went to the main staircase, and started climbing. Boyd watched her. With one hand, she held on to the banister. Her back was straight, her hips swayed. Her high, round rump was outlined against the skirt. The hem rode up, baring her booted ankles.

At the top of the stairs she paused, hand on the stair post. She glanced back over her shoulder, a meaningful glance, before continuing on her way.

Boyd went outside and around to the back of the hotel. He was in a deserted side street. Lamps burning behind curtained windows in the hotel filled the space with a soft glow. From the main square came the sound of voices, laughter. It faded, went away.

Wind blew. The moon came out from behind a cloud, shining into the side street. Boyd felt wild, spooky. A good kind of spooky. His blood sang.

He entered the stairwell, climbed to the top of the stairs. Beyond lay a short passage, joining the main hall at right angles. Boyd peeked around the corner. The long hall was floored with red carpets and lined on both sides by closed doors. Lights shone out beneath some of them. The walls had dark brown wooden wainscoting. Wall lamps shed a glow the color of old bronze.

The hall was empty. Noises, muted talk sounded from behind the doors along the corridor. Nothing indicated that any of the guests were about to step into the hall.

Discretion was necessary to avoid compromising the lady's reputation.

Boyd stepped into the hall. The first door on his right bore the identifying numerals 14.

He knocked, lightly. His face burned. He felt restless, edgy.

The door was opened so quickly that the person inside had to have been sitting right beside it, awaiting his knock. It opened a crack, as wide as the chain would allow.

A pair of long-lashed gray eyes, female eyes, looked out at him.

"Shhh!" she said.

The door closed, the chain was removed, the door

opened. Inside was a teenage girl, a pale brunette in a maid's uniform. She motioned him in, easing the door closed after he entered, locking and chaining it.

He said, "Drusilla?"

She nodded, smiling. Her hair was thick, black, coarse, the ends blunt-cut. It was cut in bangs across her forehead and down past her shoulders on the sides. She was pretty, in an unkempt way. Her eyes were knowing and her smile sly. Her eyes were wide, heavy-lidded. Her lips were dark red, almost plum-colored, naturally so, without rouge. On the top of her head was a white lace maid's cap. She wore a long-sleeved black uniform dress, a white apron, black stockings, black shoes. The apron was smudged with her lace collar and cuffs were wilted. The shiny fabric of her dress pressed tightly against her high, pert breasts.

This modest corner room was Drusilla's. A connecting door opened on Room 12, a far more grandiose suite of rooms occupied by Lydia Crane.

Drusilla opened the door, then stood with her back to it, hands reaching behind her to rest on the doorknob. She gestured to Boyd to enter. He went through the doorway into the room beyond.

He was in a kind of drawing room. The windows were curtained. There was a divan, some armchairs, a drum-shaped table with a lamp on it, and, in a corner, a writing desk and a high-backed armless chair. The Oriental rug was richly patterned with intricate red, blue, and gold designs and was bordered with gold fringe.

On the other side of the room, framed by a doorway, stood Lydia Crane. A belted black silk robe hugged her from shoulders to ankles. Beneath it was something sheer and clingy in black lace. Her legs were bare. She wore red slippers with one-inch heels. In one hand, she held a glass filled with dark brown-red fluid. Some of her hair had been unpinned, the strands hanging down like champagne-colored ribbons.

"Thank you, Drusilla," she said. "That will be all. Good night."

Drusilla nodded, backing out of the room, closing the door.

Lydia went to the door and locked it.

"She likes to watch," Lydia Crane said. "She's a wicked one."

She crossed to the open doorway, Boyd following her through it into the next room.

Inside, there was a big brass bed, cabinets, a chest of drawers, bedside night tables, a vanity with a mirror and bench. In a corner nook stood a small table and two chairs. Curtains were drawn, but the windows were open. Breezes stirred the curtains, billowing them.

Lydia Crane stood facing him, holding her glass chest-high.

"What're you drinking?" Boyd said.

"Brandy," she said. "Want some?"

"I want some," Boyd said, moving toward her.

She downed the brandy in one gulp, reaching behind her to set the glass down on the night table.

Boyd reached for her. Her body was toned, strong, vibrant. She pressed against him. He kissed her on the mouth. It tasted of brandy, sweet yet burning on his tongue.

She was a handful. He came up for air, still holding her. He kissed her neck, working his way down. He buried his face in the tops of her breasts. She held his head with both hands, winding her fingers in his hair.

He backed her to the bed. Her legs folded and she sat down. He followed, bearing her down onto her back, stretching on top of her. She writhed under him, grinding her hips, rubbing against him.

He lay on his side, an arm under the back of her head, cradling it. Her eyes were slits, moist and dreamy. Color blazed in her cheeks. Ripe lips parted.

His free hand undid the knotted belt, opening her robe. Black silk wings parted, spreading to the side. Beneath, she wore some sheer, gauzy black wrapper, the slinky fabric molded to her form. He fondled her breasts, pulling down the lace cups, baring them. They were pear-shaped, with pink button nipples. Pale pink. He squeezed, licked, and sucked them.

She squirmed, buttocks clenched, thighs pressed closed. His hands slid down her taut, slightly rounded belly to her pubis. He put his hand between her thighs and rubbed her sex through her garment.

He raised the hem, lifting it to her waist, baring her below. No undergarments clothed her nudity. She was a real blonde. Her bush was sand-colored. Between the lips of her slit, moisture glimmered.

Her hands were on him, tugging at his clothes. He

shucked off his shirt, tossed it aside. He pulled down his pants. She grasped his hardness with both hands.

He was naked enough. The woman lay on her back, breasts bared. Her middle was banded by the bunched-up black nightie. Below the waist she was nude. She still wore the black silk robe. It lay under her, like a blanket, contrasting with her white flesh.

Boyd mounted her. She clutched his shoulders. He guided himself into her and entered her. Her grip tightened convulsively. They went at it hard and fast. A hot, sweaty fuck.

The bed creaked, jiggled, jounced. Boyd held back to keep from making too much noise. Beneath him, Lydia Crane wriggled like a snake. He glued his mouth to hers. He came like an express train.

That first time took the sharp edge off his hunger. Now he could slow down and take his time. He and the woman stripped, shedding every stitch until they were buck naked. Her arms circled his neck as he climbed back in the saddle.

Later, they rested. They lay on their backs, side by side, their only cover a sheet pulled up to their waists.

She rolled on her side, facing him, resting her head on her hand. "Mind if I ask you a personal question?"

"Go ahead," he said.

Her finger traced spirals in the hair of his chest.

"What's it like to kill a man?"

"Work," he said. "A job, that's all."

"Sure," she said, openly skeptical.

"It's no more to me than driving a nail is to a carpenter," he said.

"I don't believe you," she said. "You wouldn't do it if you didn't have a passion for it."

He shrugged. "Now it's my turn to ask you something."

"Personal question?"

"Um."

"Ask away," she said.

"What's it like to fuck a man to death?" Boyd said.

"Let's find out," she said.

Her nipples were hard. She reached under the sheet, squeezing him. He throbbed in her hand, stiffening. She sat up, the sheet sliding off her. She knelt with her legs folded under her. She lowered her head to him, her mouth hot, devouring . . .

Before first light, he got out of bed and got dressed. A few lone birds chirped somewhere in the graying night.

"The ride's just begun, cowboy," she said.

She let him out through the connecting door, into Room 14. Drusilla lay on a couch, under a blanket. When the door opened, she threw her feet on the floor and rose. The maid's cap and apron lay on a nearby chair. She wore the uniform, unbuttoned at throat and collar. She stepped into a pair of slippers and went to the door.

She went outside, checking that the coast was clear. It was. From across the room, Lydia Crane blew a kiss to Boyd. He waved so long and exited.

Drusilla went inside, closing the door.

Boyd went down the back stairs, somewhat wobble-legged.

"Some night! Whew!" he said to himself.

Later that day, he had lunch with his brother.

"Seems the lady's rep is a mite overblown, Boyd," he said.

"How's that?"

"You're still alive."

That afternoon, Lydia Crane rented a house outside of town. Drusilla went on ahead to prepare it for occupancy, while her mistress finalized the business dealings that had necessitated the trip. Drusilla returned to town and spent the night in the hotel, as did Lydia Crane.

The next day, in the morning, Lydia Crane, Drusilla, and their luggage were transported to the house. Located on a knoll overlooking the town, the house stood alone, with no nearby neighbors. It was a modest one-story wooden frame house, white-painted, with four rooms. It was drab but clean.

After dark, Boyd rode out to the house. A big yellow half-moon lit the ribbon of road that wound through the countryside. Lights showed in the windows of the house. Boyd rode into the yard, dismounted.

He knocked, the door opened. Lydia Crane was waiting. Her hair was long and loose. She wore a short, dark jacket, a shiny green satin blouse, and a long skirt. She and Boyd went into a clinch. Her mouth was warm, sweet, urgent. She pressed against him. Something hard and metallic pressed against his thigh. It was a pistol in her pocket, a short-barreled revolver.

"A woman alone has to take care of herself, darling," she said.

He put the gun aside and again embraced her. This time she fit much better. Soon she felt something hard of his pressing against her thighs. It wasn't a pistol.

One of the benefits of a small house was that the bedroom wasn't very far away. Boyd swept Lydia Crane off her feet, holding her. She wrapped her arms around his neck and rested her cheek against his chest. His heart was beating fast. He carried her across the room. She felt light in his arms.

There was a front room, two bedrooms, and a kitchen. Drusilla was in the kitchen, dawdling listlessly over her chores. She was sulky, pouting. She looked up, seeing Boyd carry Lydia Crane into the bedroom.

Here there were no neighbors, no strangers in the next room to inhibit the full force of the lovemaking, as there had been at the hotel. Drusilla was here, but her tender sensibilities (if any) didn't count. Boyd and Lydia Crane went at it like cats in heat.

Boyd thrust into her as if to hammer her through the bed. She was taut with excitement, bands of muscle standing out against shiny, sweat-drenched pink flesh. She clawed Boyd's shoulders and upper back. Her face was strained, with slitted eyes and open, moaning mouth. The bed shook, moving around on the floor. The headboard slammed against the wall.

Boyd kept pouring it on. Each thrust sent the head-board cracking against the wall. It sounded like a carpenter hard at work.

Lydia bent her legs at the knees, hugging his sides. Boyd put his hand under her ass, clutching her buttocks, squeezing them. He tilted her pelvis to the optimum angle for his thrusts. She reached behind her, bracing herself, bending her wrists and pressing her palms against the headboard.

Wham!—Wham!—Wham! The headboard pounded the wall, opening a crack in the plaster. The lovers kept at it. More cracks shot through the wall, making a spidery pattern. Pieces of plaster broke off and fell to the floor.

Then, climax. Boyd raised his upper body, burying himself deep inside her. They spasmed.

The pounding stopped, bringing a sudden silence. The lovers panted, gasping for breath. Their limbs were a sweaty tangle.

A final chunk of plaster, hanging by a thread, fell to the floor . . .

Boyd and Lydia had both entered into their association with their eyes open. There was no question of love and marriage. Maybe that's what made the sex so good. It was an erotic liaison between two hot-blooded, high-powered specimens of mental and physical excellence.

Boyd stayed the night. Between the bouts of sex, there was plenty of drinking. Among the supplies were a case of brandy and a case of whiskey. She drank the former, he the latter. There was food, too, but that wasn't as high a priority.

Day and night melted together. Much of the time, Boyd and Lydia wore no clothes. When he left the bedroom for one reason or another, Boyd pulled on a pair of pants. Lydia would throw a robe over her nakedness, the sheer black silk molding to her curves. With the robe belted, held together at the waist, a *V* of pink flesh showed, from the hollow of her throat, down to the inner curves of her breasts. The silk made her nipples hard, causing them to stick out against the fabric. Below the waist, the robe flared out, baring her inner thighs.

Drusilla was always about, a sly, silent, knowing presence. Lydia became careless about closing the door. On a hot, still afternoon, Boyd took her again. Her eyes were closed. She was moaning. A blur of motion flickered in the corner of Boyd's eye. He looked up and saw Drusilla looking in through the bedroom door.

She stood leaning against the outside wall, which hid most of her body. Only her face, peeking around the corner, and her hand, clutching the door frame, could be seen. Her eyes were moist. Red dots of color showed in her cheeks. Absently she chewed on a strand of hair that fell across her face.

Surprise threw Boyd off his rhythm, and he stopped stroking. Moaning impatiently, her eyes closed, Lydia wriggled under him. She grabbed his hips and pulled him into her.

Mentally shrugging, Boyd went back to doing what

he was doing. If Drusilla wanted to watch, he'd give her a show.

When he looked up again, after the throes of a shuddering climax, Drusilla was gone.

Not far. He could hear her in the kitchen, rattling pots and pans.

The next day Boyd went to town to take care of some errands. He was tired, with dark circles under his eyes.

His brother said, "You're looking a mite peaked. This city life must be getting to you!"

Boyd smiled wanly. His brother didn't know that he'd been shacked up with Lydia Crane for the last few days, in a house rented for that purpose. Or if he did know he tactfully kept his mouth shut about it. What was important to him was that Lydia Crane's association business had been successfully transacted, to the mutual satisfaction of both parties.

Boyd bought some fresh groceries and took them out to the house, arriving after dark. In his absence, Lydia Crane had been hitting the bottle pretty good. Drusilla had been drinking, too.

Boyd had a lot of catching up to do. He cracked a fresh bottle of whiskey and went to work.

Drusilla made dinner and the three of them ate it. It was a hot autumn night. Windows were open, but not a breath of a breeze stirred the curtains. Outside, an insect chorus chirped, buzzed, clicked, and hummed, making an unholy racket.

In the front room, a single lamp burned low. Boyd sat on the couch. He wore jeans. He was shirtless and barefoot. A sheen of sweat glistened on his body. Lydia Crane sat on the couch, bare legs folded. Under black silk, she was naked. Heat—and brandy—flushed her face and the top of her chest with a rosy hue.

The air was thick with the smells of sweat, booze, tobacco smoke.

Across from the couch, on an armchair, sat Drusilla. She wore a thin black dress and was barefoot. The dress was open at the collar and the sleeves were rolled up past her elbows. She held a glass of brandy in both hands in her lap. From time to time she sipped it. She sat up very straight against the back of the chair, with her knees together and her feet on the floor. From under glazed, heavy-lidded eyes, she seemed to be watching the proceedings from a distance.

Lydia Crane drained the last few drops of brandy from the bottle into her glass. Drusilla set down her glass on the table beside her, rose, and padded into the kitchen, returning with a new bottle.

Not looking, Lydia Crane stretched out her arm, holding the empty glass. Drusilla filled it with brandy.

"Thank you, dear," Lydia Crane said. "See how she anticipates my every whim, Boyd?"

"Um," Boyd said.

"Come here," Lydia Crane said.

Drusilla moved beside her. Lydia Crane's arm encircled the girl's waist.

"She's a dear girl," Lydia Crane said. "You like her, don't you, Boyd?"

"Sure," he said guardedly.

Lydia Crane patted Drusilla's hip. She rested her cheek against the girl's other hip. Her eyes rolled, and she held on tight to keep from falling.

That was when Boyd knew she was drunk. She could hold her liquor well, better than most men, but this time she was pretty far gone. Her glazed eyes swam in and out of focus.

"You must be hot in that dress, Drusilla," she said. "Take it off."

Drusilla looked down at her, her face expressionless.

"Go on," Lydia said.

Drusilla unbuttoned her dress and took it off, pulling it up over her head. Beneath it she wore a thin white one-piece shift, with shoulder straps and a hemline below the knees.

Turning her back, she took off her shift, putting it on the table where her dress lay. Her skin was white. She was thin, and her ribs showed. There was a roundness at her hips, which were covered by a loose-fitting pair of thin white cotton drawers. The seat clung to the crack of her ass, outlining her buttocks.

Lydia Crane clutched the girl's hip and turned her so she faced front. Drusilla's arms were crossed in front of her breasts, but there was nothing coy about her expression. It was bold, intent.

"She's so shy," Lydia Crane said. "Like hell! She's just doing that to excite you."

"It's working pretty good," Boyd said.

Lydia Crane smirked. She took hold of Drusilla's

wrists and lowered the girl's arms to her sides. Her breasts were small, pert, conical, with pointy dark brown nipples.

Lydia Crane said, "Want to play? All three of us?"

"If that's what you want," Boyd said.

She put her hand on his lap, squeezing the hardness that tented the front of his jeans.

"What you want," she said.

"What about her? What does she want?" Boyd said.

"She wants what I want," Lydia Crane said. "Show him, Drusilla."

Drusilla unknotted the drawstring of her drawers and pulled them down, off her hips. They fell down her legs to her ankles. She had bony hips and a black tufted bush as sleek as an otter pelt.

She stepped out of her drawers. Lydia caught her by the wrist, pulling her down on the couch between herself and Boyd.

She pushed Drusilla toward him.

"You know what to do," she said. Boyd didn't know if she was speaking to him, or to Drusilla, or to the both of them.

Boyd embraced Drusilla. The girl seemed not unwilling. He pulled her onto his lap, her ass pressing against his hardness. He went to kiss her on the mouth. She turned her head away.

"Not on the mouth," Lydia said. "That's one of the rules. Kiss her anywhere but there."

"If that's how you want it . . ." Boyd said.

"That's the way of it," Lydia Crane said.

He stroked Drusilla's back. She leaned into it, arching her back, tilting her head. He put his hands between her thighs. They were damp with sweat. He rubbed her between the legs. She was moist there, too. She ground her pelvis against his hand. He kissed and licked her breasts. The nipples stood out like pebbles, glistening with saliva.

Lydia Crane crouched on the couch, legs doubled under her. She leaned forward, her hot-eyed, avid face leaning over the curve of Drusilla's shoulder.

"Get him ready for me," she breathed.

Drusilla disengaged from Boyd's embrace, sliding off his lap to the floor. He took off his pants. Drusilla knelt between his legs, licking her lips. He put a hand on her head and pulled it down to him.

Her hair flared across the tops of his thighs. Her head bobbed, cheeks hollowed, mouth sucking.

Lydia Crane's robe was open, baring her breasts. She tweaked and squeezed her nipples. Her other hand rubbed between her legs.

She got up, shrugging off the robe. She was unsteady on her feet, swaying. She put her hand on Drusilla's forehead and pulled back, disconnecting her from Boyd.

Drusilla moved aside. Lydia Crane faced Boyd, straddling him. Her nipples were hard, her sex was wet. He held his manhood upright, while she lowered herself down on it.

As it filled her, her eyes rolled up in her head so only the whites showed. She leaned back, almost losing her balance, but he checked her, pulling her back to him, holding her impaled. He held her under the arms, allowing him to guide and steady her movements. She bounced up and down on him, her breasts jiggling, except when he fastened his mouth on them.

Drusilla climbed onto the couch, sprawling half on, half off it. She lay on her side, facing Boyd and Lydia. She watched, fondling herself between the legs.

Lydia Crane came, breath hissing out snakelike from between clenched teeth. A deep red flush colored her front from forehead to navel. Boyd grunted.

Drusilla vented high-pitched little mewling noises.

Sated, Lydia Crane eased off him, moving as if her bones had turned to liquid. Boyd was still half-hard. It wouldn't take much to get him fired up and ready for more.

He reached for Drusilla.

"I'll finish you off right, girl," he said.

Again, she seemed willing. But Lydia Crane sat up and gripped Boyd's shoulder, sinking her fingers in.

"No," she said. "Drusilla's a good girl. She's saving it for marriage."

Boyd patted Drusilla's ass and focused his attention on Lydia Crane.

"That'll be all, Drusilla," she said. "Go to your room."

Showing neither pleasure or resentment, Drusilla got up, picked up her clothes, and went to her room.

Boyd's blood was running hot. A lull in the action was filled by drinking. Later, he bent Lydia Crane facedown across the back of the couch. Her round ass was pink and shining. Between her legs was the hairy mound. Standing behind her, he took her from behind. He held her hips while he plowed her, her buttocks jiggling. She went weak in the knees. Her legs folded, but the couch held her in place. Boyd kept putting it to her. Back arched, head tilted back, she drummed her fists against the couch, rising on tiptoes for the final thrust.

Drusilla stood just inside the doorway, peeking out behind the almost-closed door, watching . . .

Boyd woke to grayness. The windows in the house were kept constantly curtained, creating a zone where night and day blended together. It had been a wild night. Lydia Crane lay sprawled on the bed, apparently in deep sleep. Boyd shook his head to clear it. He lifted the curtain and looked outside. It was after first light but before dawn.

He needed a drink, but all the bottles in the bedroom were empty. He pulled on his pants and went into the front room. There was a rattling in the kitchen. He stuck his head in. Drusilla was up and dressed and doing chores.

Their eyes met. Boyd entered the kitchen. Drusilla got on her hands and knees and crawled to him. She pressed her face to his crotch. Even through denim he could feel her hot breath.

He stroked her head. Her nuzzlings became more urgent. He opened his pants and fed her. She took him deep into her mouth. Her head bobbed, lips and tongue working.

The moment of truth neared.

"Damn you!"

The outraged voice was Lydia Crane's. She hadn't been sleeping so soundly after all. She was naked and wrathful.

Startled, Drusilla pulled her head back, freeing Boyd.

Lydia Crane shouldered past him.

"What the hell—!?" he said.

"Going behind my back! I don't like that," Lydia Crane said. "And Drusilla knows it, the little bitch!"

She grabbed a handful of Drusilla's hair and pulled it.

"Oww!" Drusilla squealed.

"Take it easy," Boyd began.

Lydia Crane whirled on him. "It's none of your business, so keep out of it!"

Wanting no part of it, Boyd backed off, making as dignified a retreat as he could under the circumstances.

He went into the front room, standing idly by as Lydia Crane took Drusilla by the arm and marched her into the bedroom.

The door slammed.

Boyd sat down on the couch. The rhythm of Lydia Crane's angry words rose and fell, muffled by the walls.

"Hell with it," Boyd said.

He stretched out on his back on the couch, covering his eyes with an arm. It was cooler in the front room than it had been in the bedroom. He guessed he was still pretty drunk. He fell asleep.

A racket woke him, the sound of agonized cries and repeated blows coming from the bedroom.

The door wasn't locked. Inside, Lydia Crane was whipping Drusilla. The woman wore tan riding breeches and knee-high brown leather boots. Above the waist, she was naked. Her eyes glittered and her color was high. In one hand she held a leather belt, doubled.

Drusilla knelt on the bed with her head down and her ass up. Her dress was bunched at her waist and her drawers were down at her knees. Her hands lay on either side of her head, fingers clawing the bedsheets. Her ass was crisscrossed with angry red welts.

Boyd grabbed Lydia Crane's wrist, stopping her before she could deliver another blow.

"You crazy—?!" he cried.

Defiant, glaring, she laughed a brittle laugh. Boyd was unprepared for what happened next.

Drusilla whirled, her face rabid. She flew at Boyd, fingernails tearing at his eyes. He fended her off. She screeched like a hoot owl. He held her by the wrists, her nails ripping empty air. She tried to knee him.

"Don't hurt her!" Lydia Crane said.

Boyd flung Drusilla away from him, onto the bed. She crawled across it, lunging toward a night table on the other side. She flung open a drawer, hands scrabbling inside it.

She came up with a gun.

"Drusilla, don't!" Lydia Crane cried.

Boyd threw himself to the floor. Shots rang out, passing overhead.

Lydia Crane rushed Drusilla. She bent the girl's wrist, pointing the gun at the ceiling. Another shot exploded harmlessly before the gun was in Lydia Crane's hand.

Drusilla's eyes bulged. Her face was chalk-white. Lydia Crane slapped her, hard. The room rang with the impact of the blow. Drusilla's head was knocked to the side. Lydia Crane backhanded her. She slapped Drusilla down until the girl collapsed in hysterics on the bed.

Coming up behind Lydia Crane, Boyd plucked the gun from her hand.

"I better hold on to this," he said.

Lydia Crane sat down beside the sobbing girl, gathering her in her arms, pulling her head to her breast. Drusilla's cheeks flared hot red with the imprint of Lydia Crane's striking hand. She buried her tear-stained face in the woman's bosom. Lydia Crane stroked her head, smoothing her hair, murmuring tender consolations.

Daylight shone through the bullet holes in the wall.

Boyd shook his head. "The game's getting too rich for my blood."

Lydia Crane left off her strokings of Drusilla long enough to look up.

"End of the ride, cowboy," she said. "It was fun while it lasted, but it got out of hand."

Boyd dressed quickly, throwing his few personal belongings in a bag. He went outside and saddled his horse.

Lydia Crane came out the front door, buttoning the

blouse that she had thrown on.

"Hope there's no more guns inside," Boyd said.

"She's all right," Lydia Crane said. "Now."

"Now that I'm leaving, you mean."

She shrugged. "Drusilla's young, impulsive."

"So was Billy the Kid," Boyd said.

He gave her the pistol and the two remaining shells he had unloaded from it. "Keep these away from the girl until I'm out of shooting range, please."

"I will." She pocketed guns and shells.

"A hell of a ride at that," he said.

She smiled. He stepped into the saddle.

"Adios," he said.

She nodded. He urged the horse forward.

At the side of the house, curtains parted to reveal Drusilla standing at the window, her face a pale oval. Boyd got ready to duck. She waved in farewell.

He waved so long, shaking his head in wry wonderment.

Lydia Crane turned and went into the house, closing the door. She came up behind Drusilla, still standing at the window. She put her hands on the girl's shoulders and led her away.

The curtains fell, veiling the window.

That same day, Lydia Crane and her maid left Abilene. Boyd told his brother he was ready to go back to work. It took a week on the trail before he had dried out and cleared the cobwebs from his head.

Time passed, leaving him with the memory of a wild bender. It was succeeded by other women, other benders. His nature was to look ahead, not dwelling overmuch on the past.

A year passed, more. Then came the day, six weeks ago, when Boyd's brother dumped the Shatter Valley murders in his lap.

"Who's the association's man up there?" Boyd said.

"Dunne," his brother said. "He's good, but running down a kill-crazy band of renegades is out of his line."

"But it's in my line, huh?"

"Yes," his brother said. "Dunne requested you personally, by name."

"Never met the man," Boyd said.

"Well, he's heard of you," his brother said. "Courtesy of an area rancher who convinced him you're the man for the job."

"Who's that?"

"You knew her. Lydia Crane," his brother said.

Six

THUNK.

It was the sound of a counterweight being thrown, a trap being sprung; a heavy sound. Muted, but deep, ponderous.

Click.

Hard on the heels of the thud, as if in echo, came the click. Lighter, more delicate than the first noise, it had a mechanical quality, as of gears shifting or a spring being released.

Hairs rose on the back of Boyd's neck. A sense of imminent danger seized him.

His thoughts were heavy, slow. That was part of the danger, he knew, yet he didn't know how he knew it. His eyes were closed. Had he been sleeping? That was bad. He wasn't the man for sleeping on watch.

He didn't remember falling asleep. The last thing he remembered was sitting in front of the fire, thinking about Abilene and his brother and Lydia Crane and how they had all come together to bring him on association business to Shatter Valley and Packer Point Station.

His body felt inert, leaden. His limbs were cold and tingling. His head hurt and there was a bad taste in his mouth.

He remained motionless, piecing things together. He had fallen asleep and something had wakened him. What?

A noise—noises—*THUNK,* and *click.*

The first had come from behind him, the second, from somewhere on his left.

Opening his eyes was an effort. The lids felt all gluey. He opened them to slits, seeing little more than vague forms of shadow and light.

Immediately his headache multiplied tenfold, hammering his skull from the inside. He stifled a groan. It was important to play possum, deadly important, though he wasn't sure why.

He felt bad, sick. Queasy, his skin clammy. His head throbbed, pounding until it felt like it was about to split.

His eyes widened, taking in more of the scene. It was dizzying. The room seemed to spin. It went in and out of focus. He concentrated, and the spasm passed.

He still sat at the table in the big room. The glass lay on its side on the tabletop, beside a puddle of spilled fluid.

The room was dark, much darker than it had been. The fire had burned down low. He couldn't see it, it was behind his back. No heat came off it. Reflected firelight on the ceiling was reduced to a few sluggish red strands wriggling through murky shadows, like eels burrowing into river-bottom muck.

His heart pounded.

Now there was another noise, a new sound. A faint scraping sound.

A subtle thing happened, a slight disturbance in the currents of the air. Firelight flickered, flaring up.

The scraping continued. The light brightened. It was not bright, it was too low for that, but the dimness lessened.

In one quick motion Boyd grabbed the shotgun, closed it, half rose out of his chair, and pivoted, swinging the shotgun around to the left behind him.

A quick glimpse—

A man was coming out of the hearth. A stunted, twisted figure, with huge shoulders and arms and shrunken, bandy legs.

The dwarf.

On his face was an expression of fiendish malignancy. In his hand was a knife.

The interior of the fireplace was six feet high, five feet wide, and six feet deep. The rear wall was hinged, mounted on a vertical center axis. It jutted open and outward at a forty-five-degree angle, disclosing a blank black space behind it.

From this space the dwarf had just emerged. The sound of the mechanism operating the secret door had stirred Boyd into wakefulness. The scraping was the sound of the door opening. The change in pressure had disturbed the air, making the fire flare up.

The dwarf was edging around the embers, out from under the mantel. Red light underlit his face, a jack-o'-lantern face carved in a fleshy pumpkin head. His eyes were triangular rattlesnake eyes, bright with scarlet gleams.

Boyd was clumsy, slower than usual, but he had the drop on the dwarf. He didn't even wait to enjoy it. He cut loose with both barrels.

Nothing happened, except for two clicks when he pulled the triggers.

The dwarf's arm flashed up and down, firelight glinting on the blade in his hand.

Boyd threw himself to the side, crashing to the floor. The knife missed, pinwheeling across the room, clattering on the floorboards.

The dwarf leaped, jumping high up in the air. He came down with his knees bent, trying to crush Boyd's chest.

Boyd took the impact on his bent forearms, throwing the dwarf off. The dwarf rolled, got his feet under him, and lunged at Boyd, diving across the floor.

Boyd still held the shotgun. He slashed sideways, slamming the butt at the dwarf's head. The dwarf raised his hands to block. They were as big as cooking mittens, the fingers talons.

The shotgun butt smashed him in the face, but a hand was in the way, cushioning the impact. There was a wet, smacking sound. The dwarf's head rocked.

Momentum carried the dwarf forward, on top of Boyd. With his good hand, the dwarf grabbed the gun stock. Boyd reversed, slashing in the opposite direction, raking the shotgun barrels against the dwarf's face.

There was a satisfying crunch of metal against bone. The blow fell on the right side of the dwarf's face, bruising the flesh above the eye. Boyd struck again in the same spot, opening a cut.

But the second blow was far weaker than the first, now that the dwarf had tightened his one-handed grip on the gun. His upper body strength was immense, ape-ish. His shoulders were as broad as an axe handle is long, slabbed with mounds of ropy muscle. His arms were pythons.

His maimed hand flopped down on the shotgun, clamping it with a crablike pincer grip. Boyd held the shotgun in both hands, horizontally above his chest. He pushed up. The dwarf pushed down.

Blood from the cut trickled into the dwarf's right eye. It made him look more maniacal, if possible. Without straining, he overcame Boyd's resistance, flattening the shotgun across his chest. Spittle from his panting mouth spattered Boyd's face, stinging like venom.

The dwarf bucked, pressing down with his hands, putting his weight on the shotgun, crushing Boyd. His lower body lifted up and came down with the legs doubled, trying to pulp Boyd's groin.

Boyd blocked with his thigh, absorbing the blow and the quick flurry that followed. His thigh was going numb.

He snuggled his chin at his chest, forestalling the

dwarf's attempt to wedge the shotgun against the soft parts of his throat.

All Boyd's movements were defensive. That was no good. He had to take the play away from the dwarf.

Boyd grabbed the crooked index finger of the dwarf's bad hand, bending it backward until it broke.

The dwarf grunted, his grip weakening. Boyd kept up the pressure, bending the finger more, grinding the broken bone against the socket.

The dwarf howled, let go. Now he was off balance, if only for an instant. Boyd levered the gun butt, delivering a smashing uppercut to the underside of the dwarf's chin.

He thrust the gun butt into the dwarf's throat, grinding, crushing.

"Grrrr," the dwarf said.

Boyd pried the dwarf up and off him. The dwarf hit the floor, bouncing up like a rubber ball. Boyd got to his feet, staggering forward. The dwarf rolled upright, legs doubled under him. They uncoiled, propelling him headfirst in a leaping lunge at Boyd.

Boyd met him halfway, buttstroking him in the face, stopping him in midair. He hit the dwarf so hard that the recoil shivered through him from head to toe.

The dwarf flopped to hands and knees, split face hanging down, hands scrabbling at Boyd's feet.

Boyd slammed the shotgun down, hitting the dwarf in the side of the head. The dwarf hit the floor face down.

"Grrrr, grrrr," he said.

A groping hand found Boyd's foot, closed on it. The dwarf squirmed forward, head darting, fastening his jaws around the boot, chomping at the ankle underneath.

Boyd kicked free. He kicked the other's head, kept kicking it. Clawing hands tore at his feet. He stomped the hands. Squashed flat, they seemed as big across as dinner plates.

He put the toe of a boot under the dwarf and rolled him on his back. The dwarf lay there, limbs thrashing, teeth gnashing, like an upended snapping turtle.

Boyd thrust the gun butt between the jaws, into the mouth, and down the throat. He bore down, twisting it back and forth.

The dwarf's spine snapped. He convulsed, died.

From start to finish, the fight had lasted less than sixty seconds.

If Boyd had felt poorly before—and he had—it was nothing compared to the way he felt now. Only heart-pumping adrenaline kept him on his feet.

He shouldn't be on his feet. He made a better target that way. He drew his gun, the first chance he'd had to do so since the fracas began.

He went to the floor, lying prone, gun cocked and aimed at the door behind the fireplace.

His breathing was loud in his ears.

The rest was silence.

That was bad. A knock-down-drag-out fight like the one he just engaged in should have waked others from their slumbers. Where were they?

The black oblong where the door in the fireplace

opened remained empty, untenanted.

Boyd crawled to the left of the hearth, wriggling on his belly out of the line of fire. The secret passage still looked empty. He sat up, legs stretched out, widening his focus. The hidden door was the most obvious source of threat, but danger could come from any direction.

He scanned the room, starting at the hearth and working counterclockwise, his gaze sweeping along the left wall, over tables and chairs, through the open center space of the floor, beyond into the main hall, continuing to the long side wall.

When his gaze came to the wall on the right of the kitchen door, it stopped.

Mora Tanner stood with her back flattened against the wall. She wore only a long-sleeved white flannel nightgown, with a lace collar and cuffs, its hem brushing her ankles. She wore dark socks. She was stiff, rigid. Every muscle was tensed, standing out against her nightgown. Her neck was corded, her jaws were knotted, and pencil-thick veins bulged at the sides of her forehead. Her arms were held away from her sides, palms pressing the wall, fingers splayed.

Not only Boyd's gaze but also his gun was trained on her. He didn't know what he would have done if her hands hadn't been empty. The way her long, coltish form was outlined against the flannel nightgown, there was no room for concealed weapons.

Her eyes were like a caged bird's. They made contact with his. She giggled.

Boyd put a finger across his lips. ''Shhhh.''

He didn't know if she got it or not, but there were no more giggles.

He rose, crouching. Before anything else, he wanted a look inside that secret door. Gun in hand, he angled crabwise to the looming fireplace, covering behind a corner edge.

Cold, dank air wafted out of the passageway, stirring loose ashes from the embers mounded in the center of the hearth. Boyd approached as if walking on eggs. He didn't know who or what lay beyond the threshold of the secret door.

He kept a wary eye on Mora, too. She stayed glued to the same spot, standing on tiptoe and shivering.

The fire was low, the stone walls cool. Boyd ducked his head under the mantel, edging toward the opening. He held his gun at his side, leveled, instead of holding it out at arm's length where somebody could take it.

The secret panel was about a foot thick. Through its center was a vertical metal pole, the ends sunk into the top and bottom of the frame. When the catch was released, a system of hidden counterweights caused the door to swing open on its axis.

Boyd sidestepped through the opening, ready to blast.

He stood alone, on a stone square smaller than the hearth floor. It was the top landing of a stone staircase. A spiral staircase. The space enclosing the landing was about as roomy as a closet. The ceiling was low. Pale, hazy light filtered in from outside. The space was dim, almost dark.

Boyd didn't want to get too far from the door for fear that it might close. He leaned over the top of the stairs, looking down into the well. The stairs wound their way downward along the circular shaft.

From below came a smell of dampness, wet stone and earth, stagnant pools, slime, and rotten meat. About ten feet down, an indirect light cast a glow on the curving wall. It shone out of the mouth of a side passage. It was stationary, motionless.

The only sound was that of water dripping somewhere in the depths.

Boyd backed off. No doubt a mechanism existed by which the door could be opened or closed from this side. A lever, wheel, or protruding stud. A quick look failed to reveal any such switch.

He went back through the passage, into the fireplace. The room was unchanged, including Mora Tanner, who stood riveted to the same spot.

Boyd came out from under the mantel, into the open. He didn't like having that open doorway at his back, but there was no help for that now.

Somehow the table in front of the fireplace had survived the fight untouched. The lamp burned steadily and the bottle remained upright. Light glinting on the spill from the overturned glass transformed it into a puddle of liquid copper.

A bitter metallic taste clung to his tongue and mouth, suggesting certain possibilities.

He held the bottle under his nose and sniffed. Rotgut, raw fumes boiling off it. But wasn't there something else in the mix, a strong scent of something medicinal?

He put aside the bottle, an object for future investigation. The pocket watch was still ticking away. He checked the time: two-thirty-five in the morning. He was supposed to have awakened Krater at two to stand his turn at guard duty.

It occurred to Boyd that behind the bar was a good place to hide. He approached it cautiously, but no one was hiding there.

A floorboard creaked under his foot. Mora's head swiveled toward the sound. Now she faced Boyd, watching him with mad eyes.

He came on, nice and easy, making no sudden moves. He stopped when he got a good look at her feet. She wasn't wearing socks, her feet were covered with blood. Bloody footprints marked the area where she stood, leading out from the kitchen.

Boyd skirted the girl, giving her a wide berth. He didn't know what the hell she might do. If she jumped wrong, he was ready to lay his gun barrel across the side of her head. She seemed content to stay frozen in place.

Cautiously he eased his head into the main hall, which was empty. So, too, were the long corridors flanking it on either side.

He could have let go a few shots and raised a ruckus, but he didn't. Why?

The dead dwarf was answer enough. He lay on the floor, like a squashed bug. That had upset somebody's plans. Mora's being here also seemed to indicate that some part of the scheme had gone awry—or did it?

Through a glass porthole set at eye level in the swinging door, he could see into the kitchen. Not much; the angle was narrow. Inside, there was a light.

To enter the kitchen he would have to pass by Mora. He'd have liked not to get within reaching distance of her, but there didn't seem any way around it. In the west wing, off the corridor, was a back door to the kitchen, but he had no way of knowing if it was locked or not. Mora had come through the swinging door, though—the bloody footprints proved that.

He eased past Mora as gingerly as if she were a big dog that might bite. Who knew but that she might? The dwarf had. Luckily he hadn't been able to get his teeth past the boot.

He palmed the door open and went through it, stepping off to the right once he was inside.

The door swung shut behind him.

Mora was at his back.

Ahead lay the kitchen, lit by a lamp that stood on top of a butcher-block table in the center of the space. Outside the circle of light, shadows were rusty-brown.

A clean, well-ordered place. Dishes were put away, pots and pans hung on the racks, tables wiped clean, the floor swept. Bloody footprints tracked across the floor to an archway in the opposite corner of the room. There was one set of tracks, and they were going away from the archway.

Boyd soft-footed across the kitchen, avoiding the blood. Beyond the archway lay the back hall of the west wing. Light from the kitchen spilled into the hall. The hall was dark, with no light of its own, except for a pale glow shining out of the bathhouse. The footprints came out of the bathhouse.

Boyd ducked into the storeroom, flattening against the wall. The storeroom was dim, silent. There was a smell of flour and grain and canned preserves.

Boyd stepped into the hall, a gun in each hand. He went down the hall, upper body tilted to the side to present less of a target. He went to the bathhouse. The door was wide open. Nobody was hiding behind it. Boyd checked.

The room was lit by a lone candle that slouched on the cabinet, the flame guttering in a shallow pool of melted wax.

Bleekman sat in the steel tub, taking a bath.

A blood bath.

He was fully dressed, except for a hat. He was wedged into the tub sitting up, with his legs bent and his knees at his chin. A tight fit.

His throat had been cut with such force that he was nearly decapitated. His head rested on his knees. The murder weapon was nowhere in sight. Most of the blood had gone into the tub, but some had slopped over onto the boards. Mora Tanner had entered the room, stepped into a puddle of blood, and exited, leaving a trail of red footprints.

They were the only tracks. Was she the killer? Granted, the girl might have lured him to the bathhouse, for some unknowable purpose. But cut his throat? The only blood on her was what she had stepped in. It would have been some task for her to slash a full-grown adult male like Bleekman to death without getting a few drops on her nightgown. But the garment was spotless, except at the hem, and that could be explained as the result of stepping into a pool of blood.

If not Mora, who? If she were indeed innocent, then the killer had left no tracks. Which meant that Bleekman's throat had been cut after he was put in the tub. He was already dead or insensible by then. Perhaps a drugged drink had made him easier to handle. Even so, it would be no mean feat to wrestle a man of Bleekman's size and weight into the cramped tub.

What about the folder of documents? Bleekman had set a lot of store by it. Was it still on him?

Bleekman was a ghastly mess, his front drenched in blood. Boyd didn't want to get any on his hands, not out of squeamishness, but because slippery fingers made it harder to hold a gun properly. He found a long-handled brush and used it to poke around Bleekman's jacket pockets. The wound was ugly, deep. Bleekman's head jiggled as Boyd probed for the packet. Light shone off his bald spot.

The outer pockets were empty. The brush handle dipped inside a lapel, peeling it back, exposing the inside breast pocket. Jacket and shirt were blood-soaked. The pocket was empty.

The jostling caused Bleekman's head to roll off his knees. For an instant, Boyd thought the head would come completely off, but it held.

No folder.

You got in the wrong game this time, gambler, Boyd thought.

But what had Bleekman's game been?

Boyd exited. Down the hall, on the right side, was the back door to the living quarters shared by Mora and Kate Tanner. It was closed. No light shone out from under it—no, wait, there was light, a glimmer that Boyd could make out as he neared it.

Standing against the wall, he tried the doorknob, which turned freely. He took a deep breath, caught himself doing it, said the hell with it, flung open the door, and stepped in, ready to blast.

At first glance the room was empty. Two rooms, actually, with most of the dividing wall removed to make a wide, square archway. The females each had a room of her own, with free and easy access between them.

This must be Kate's room, for the clothes left carelessly lying about were too big and too bold for Mora. The bed had not been slept in. Furniture and decor were ornate, overstuffed. Tables were covered with knotted shawls on which sat an abundance of bric-a-brac. A corner on the other side of the room was hidden by a six-foot-tall screen of folding panels. There were a lot of mirrors, some antique.

In the air was a sweet smell of face powder and cosmetics. Also, a strong medicinal aroma.

Boyd searched the room, gun in hand. His gun hummed like a dowsing rod, seeking not hidden waters but hidden lurkers. He looked under the bed. Behind the screen, of course. The medicinal smell was stronger on that side of the room. He looked in a closet. In it was nothing but women's clothes. What lay behind the closet wall? A secret passage? If so, he couldn't find it.

He went into the other room, Mora's room. The bed had been slept in. The covers were thrown back, as they would be if the girl had gotten out of bed.

On a bedside night table sat a tray. On it was a glass and spoon, the spoon inside the glass. In the bottom of the glass was an inch or so of water, discolored by the stuff on the spoon. The spoon was coated with a thin brown film that smelled medicinal.

Boyd went into the other room. To the right of the archway stood a tall, darkly stained wooden cabinet. There the medicinal smell was strongest. The upper third of the cabinet was fronted by a pair of knobbed drawers. Boyd opened them. Inside, amid various other odds and ends, was a square-sided brown glass bottle with a few inches of dark brown fluid left.

It was laudanum, an opium derivative, a powerful narcotic universally dispensed, available, and legal in the society of the time.

Boyd exited into the main corridor. Across the hall was Ned Tanner's door. Stealthily, Boyd tried the knob. The door was locked. From within, not a sound.

After a while, Boyd moved off. The supply room was locked. He'd have liked a look in there.

The telegraph office door was open. The room was dark. The indoor shutters were open, uncovering the long horizontal window in the wall opposite the door. It was a black rectangle.

As far as he could tell, the telegraphic apparatus was intact, unharmed. The coils were still attached to the contact points of the operator's key.

Boyd stood against the wall on one side of the window. He crouched down, peering out the corner of the glass. There was darkness and a deeper darkness that was the train, with an island of light that shone through the shaded windows of the private car.

At the train's tail, the lights of the caboose were small, sharp crystals.

No sign of a patroling sentry. No sign of trouble, either. The sentry could be hidden from view on the far side of the train. Whose watch was it? Carr's or Megrim's? Boyd wasn't sure.

He drifted into the hall. Mora Tanner was in the same place. So was the dwarf.

Boyd considered the locked and barred front door. Was it better opened or closed? Secret passages made the station open to invasion. Locked doors were no guarantee against any number of unknown attackers literally crawling out of the walls. Conversely, they could keep out his allies on the train. If they were still alive, and able to help.

Or, opening the door might leave one more means of entry dangerously unsecured.

He let it stand, for now.

What to do about Mora? She was laudanum-drugged and in shock from finding Bleekman murdered. At best, she was unstable in the extreme, her nature and ultimate allegiances a mystery.

He went to her—not too close.

"Miss Mora," he said.

Her eyes flashed, that was all.

"Can you talk? Or are you too far gone for that?"

She turned her head toward him. Her neck was so tight it creaked. Annoyance came over her face, as if she was irked.

"Of course I can speak," she said. "I'm not some idiot, you know."

"No," he said.

"Some poor dumb beast of the field," she went on.

"No, no, of course not," he said, humoring her.

She thrust a pointing finger at the dwarf. "Not like him—it, I mean."

"You, uh, know him?"

Her gaze turned inward, becoming sly. "I know more than some people think I do."

"What's happening now?"

"Oh, they're killing," she said, as matter-of-factly as if she had said, "Oh, it's raining."

"Who is?"

"The Red Slayers," she said. "That's what I call them, after the poem. Do you know it? It's by—I forget. '*If the Red Slayer slays*'—that's how it begins. I forget the rest.

"But it reminds me of *them*. Red Slayers—that's them, all right," she said.

"Are we talking about some characters out of a poem, or real flesh-and-blood people?" Boyd said impatiently.

"Is *that* real?" Meaning the dwarf. Her tone was scathing.

"Now we're getting somewhere," Boyd said. "The dwarf—"

"Pye," she said.

"What?"

"Pye." She spelled it out. "That's his name."

"Pye, sure. How many more like him?"

"None—like him," she said.

"But there's others?"

"Oh, yes."

"How many?"

"One big happy family," she said.

The stiffness had dissolved from her body. She stood with her hands behind her back, tracing designs on the floor with her big toe.

"I got my feet wet," she said. Giggling.

From the east wing came shouts and screams.

Seven

Boyd caught Mora by the wrist, pulling her after him as he started forward.

"Come on!" he said.

He didn't know how she'd react. He was tempted to leave her behind, but he couldn't risk losing her. Whatever her role, be it as pawn or player—or hostage—she was too valuable to cede to the enemy.

Her mood changing like quicksilver, she immediately fell in with his plans, trailing him without hesitancy. Enthusiastically, as if they were gamboling on some madcap lark. She was excited, her eyes and face shining.

Boyd kept hold of her wrist anyway.

They raced down the east wing corridor. Her bare feet flashed.

She held back when they reached the middle of the hall. Muffled shrieks sounded further along it.

She stopped, digging her heels in.

Boyd let go of her and kept on going. The commotion was coming from behind the door of a room on the left, the room shared by Stubbs and Krater.

He glanced back. Mora sat in the middle of the hall, her legs tucked under her, demurely covered by her nightgown, which she held pulled down tight to her ankles.

She would keep.

The door was locked. Boyd bootheeled it, splintering the frame and sending the door crashing inward.

A few feet beyond the threshold, Stubbs crouched on the floor, his back to the door, holding his hands in front of him to protect himself. Krater was nowhere in sight.

On Stubbs's left was a bed, the covers disarranged, a length of sheets and blankets stretching downward, entangled with Stubbs's legs.

Crouched on the bed was Kate Tanner, naked but for a leather belt around her waist and a pair of moccasins. Her front was smeared with blood. In one hand, she held a foot-long butcher knife and in the other, an enormous wooden mallet.

Deeper in the room, at the foot of the bed, stood Ned Tanner, a hatchet in his hand.

His face was in shadows, all but the lenses of his spectacles, which some trick of light had turned to golden orbs. He wore a vest but no shirt. His chest sagged, his belly immense. He wore baggy pants and no shoes or socks.

Behind him, jutting into the floor at a tilted angle, stood a wardrobe cabinet that had come away from the rear wall, revealing a black doorway.

Kate Tanner moved at the same instant Boyd did, but he had only to move his trigger finger. At that, she was so quick that she got her legs doubled under her, poised for a leaping lunge.

The shot tore into her, hitting her high in the chest. The muzzle flare lit the room like lightning.

A second slug produced a satisfying thud.

The hatchet came hurtling at Boyd's head. He dodged. Ned Tanner threw himself backward into the black doorway, tumbling through it. Boyd fired at him, missed.

Ned Tanner was out of the line of fire. Kate Tanner sprawled face down across the bed, still clutching the knife. The mallet had fallen to the floor.

Boyd jockeyed for a better angle on Ned Tanner, but Stubbs was in the way. Playing possum, Kate Tanner slashed out with the knife, narrowly missing Boyd's thigh.

Bullets exploded from the black doorway, punching holes in the wall. Boyd fired back.

Stubbs grabbed the mallet with both hands and brought it down on Kate's head. She stiffened.

Beyond the black doorway, a lever thudded home.

The gap shrank, swallowed up by a solid panel that filled the frame until barely a crack showed.

Stubbs was on his knees at the side of the bed, the bedclothes still tangled around his lower legs. Kate Tanner lay unmoving. Stubbs hit her on the head again with the mallet. She stiffened, then went slack. He hit her again. She stayed slack.

Stubbs picked up the knife and stabbed her in the

back. The knife struck a shoulder blade, breaking off at the tip. The fragment struck Stubbs in the forehead, drawing blood. He touched his fingers to the wound. They came away bloody. That sobered him.

"I could have lost an eye!" he said.

Boyd went to the wall. A hairline crack denoted where the panel fit into the wall. The wall was discolored, bearing the faded outline of the wardrobe cabinet that had stood against it.

Boyd could find no way to open the panel from this side.

The wardrobe cabinet wasn't linked to any concealed mechanisms. It was just a wooden cabinet. It was light, though, and could be moved with a minimum of exertion.

He put his ear to the wall, heard nothing.

He turned his attention to the room. Opposite, two single beds lay with their heads to the wall. The one nearer the door had been Stubbs's. The other was occupied by Krater. He lay on his back, blankets covering him to his waist. His throat was cut and there were multiple stab wounds to his chest. The killing bore the hallmarks of the same savage butchery that had been inflicted on Bleekman.

Boyd went to the door and looked outside. Mora sat with her back to the wall, legs bent, knees raised, hands clamped firmly over her ears. Her eyes were squeezed shut.

Boyd went back in the room. Stubbs had managed to disentangle himself from the bedcoverings and now stood on his feet, shakily.

"My God," he said. "My God!"

He glanced at the next bed, then looked away, shaking his head.

"Poor Krater! He never had a chance. They got to him first. I woke up to the sound of him being slaughtered. I didn't know what it was . . . He didn't cry out. I guess he was choking on his own blood.

"I didn't know what was happening, but I knew it was bad. The room was dark, except for a light. That one," he said, pointing at a hand-lantern perched on top of the wardrobe cabinet.

"They brought it with them, the murdering devils," Stubbs said. "At first it was so low that you could hardly see anything. I heard Krater gasping and choking and bubbling. I said, *What's wrong*? The light got brighter. Tanner stood there, turning it up until it was bright enough to see by. They were having a little fun with me! Then I saw Krater—You sure came along at the right time," Stubbs said. "I thought I was a goner!"

"We're not out of the woods yet," Boyd said.

"Let's get out of here!"

Stubbs wore a red flannel shirt and a pair of striped denim overalls with the bib hanging down. He wrestled the straps onto his shoulders. He was bullnecked, thick-bodied. He was almost bald, except for some close-cropped gray stubble on the sides of his head. His face was square, blunt-featured. He had a charcoal-gray mustache.

He put on his shoes and a denim jacket and grabbed his kit bag off a chair. He opened it, reaching inside.

Boyd said, "Do you have a gun?"

Stubbs was struck by a revelation. He reached into his jacket pocket and pulled out a pistol.

"I forgot I had it!" he said. Then he added apologetically, "Things happened so fast, I didn't have time to think of it."

"Well, watch where you point that thing."

"Sorry. Pardon my carelessness. I'm still not myself yet," Stubbs said.

He put the gun in his pocket, patting it. "It'll keep 'til I need it."

"That might be soon," Boyd said.

Stubbs put his hand back on the gun.

"I'll tell you when," Boyd said.

From out of his bag Stubbs took a pint glass bottle. It was a little less than half full of amber liquid.

Stubbs applied his teeth to the cork and pulled it out. There was a liquid popping sound.

"I need this," he said.

"Hold it," Boyd said.

Stubbs, holding the bottle under his mouth, looked quizzically at the Boyd.

"That house whiskey?" he asked.

"Hell, no!" Stubbs shook his head. "I wouldn't drink the rotgut they sell here. This's my own private stock. Why do you ask?"

"Some of the whiskey here is drugged," Boyd said.

"Drugged! The bastards," Stubbs said. "Well, there's nothing wrong with this liquor."

He tilted the bottle and took a long pull. Years of

exposure to the outdoors had weathered his face to a ruddy bronze. Now it looked pale, bloodless.

When he lowered the bottle, some color had returned to his face.

"Nothing wrong with that," he said, wiping his mouth on the back of his hand.

He started to recork it, then paused and offered the bottle to Boyd. "Want some?"

"Sure," Boyd said.

He took a fat slug. Maybe it would help burn away some of the cobwebs left behind by the drugged whiskey.

"That's good," Boyd said.

"Private stock," Stubbs said.

He put in the cork, started to put the bottle in the bag, thought better of it, and dropped it in the side pocket of his overalls.

"Imagine that! All the time, the Tanners were the killers," he said.

"Some of them," Boyd said.

The engineer grew alarmed. "What! There's more?"

"You don't know the half of it," Boyd said.

Stubbs started for the door. Boyd caught him by the arm.

"One thing," Boyd said. "The girl's outside."

Stubbs was puzzled. "Who?"

"Mora Tanner. She's in the hall."

"What? She's one of them!"

"She's crazy, but maybe not a killer," Boyd said.

"Why take chances? The whole bunch should be wiped out!"

"She's in custody," Boyd said. "My custody."

"If that's how you want it," Stubbs said doubtfully.

They went into the hall. It was empty.

"Thought you said the girl was out here," Stubbs said.

"Damn," Boyd said. "Better get that gun out."

"Damn," Stubbs said. He fumbled the gun out of his pocket, holding it level at the hip. His hand was steady enough.

Boyd said, "If you see the girl, don't shoot."

Stubbs didn't say anything. He faced the far end of the hall, fidgeting.

"I mean it," Boyd said.

"If she comes at me with a knife, I'll shoot," Stubbs said. "These crazy bitches can kill you!"

"Fair enough," Boyd said.

He moved alongside Bleekman's door. "Cover the hall, Stubbs."

Stubbs, uneasy, said, "Why don't we get out of here?"

"To where?"

"The train."

"We don't want to go from the frying pan into the fire," Boyd said. As he spoke, he was reloading his gun. "We don't know what's outside. Could be worse than here."

"You . . . you think something happened to the others?"

"I don't know," Boyd said.

"They must have heard the shooting," Stubbs said. "They'll come to help us."

"If they can."

Flattening his back against the wall to the right of the door, his gun leveled, Boyd reached for the knob with his free hand.

Stubbs, facing west along the main corridor, looked over his shoulder to see what Boyd was doing.

"Bleekman! I forgot about him," Stubbs said.

"Keep forgetting," Boyd said.

"Huh?"

"He's dead."

"Him too?" Stubbs gulped. "Why are you going in his room?"

"To make sure it's empty," Boyd said. "Keep your eyes watching the hall."

"Right," Stubbs said.

Bleekman's room was empty. No secret doors (that Boyd could see), nobody hiding in the closet or under the bed.

The same applied to Boyd's room, which he checked next. He came out, rejoining Stubbs.

"All right," Boyd said.

They went down the aisle, toward the center hall. From outside came shouts, shots.

"The train," Stubbs whispered.

"At least some of them are alive," Boyd said. "Otherwise, no shooting.

"Unless it's a trick to lure us outside," he added after a pause.

Shots popped off like a string of firecrackers. Then, silence. A few more sporadic shots were fired, almost as if in afterthought.

Much nearer, there was a shrill scream.

"That came from inside!" Stubbs said.

Boyd was already moving. A shriek sounded, thin and wailing. It came from the big room.

As he drew abreast of the end of the corridor, Boyd dove for the floor, gun in hand. He came out of the chute like he was squirted out. He landed on his belly, momentum carrying him across the carpeted floor of the center hall in a forward slide.

In the big room, a sticklike figure held Mora Tanner under one arm, carrying her into the fireplace. The abductor was a man, bald, with pointy ears and buck teeth. His head was long. His buckskinned torso was tube-shaped. He was six and a half feet tall, with stilt-like arms and legs. He had to duck low to keep from hitting his head on the top of the fireplace.

Looking back, he sneered at Boyd. Or maybe that was just the buck teeth.

Boyd couldn't shoot at him for fear of hitting the girl.

"*Look out!*" she screamed.

A hand clamped over her mouth, silencing her. She must have bitten it, for her captor let out a howl of pain and lost his grip.

She called out, "*The kitchen—*"

The bald man knocked her head against the chimney with a thud that Boyd could hear from across the room.

The swinging door crashed open.

In the doorway stood Ned Tanner, holding a hand cannon. His fall into the secret passage in the guest room had left bruises on his head and arms. The right lens of his glasses was cracked, frosty with a spider-web pattern. Pinwheels of light glinted off it as he moved.

He charged out, looking for Boyd, not immediately seeing him on the floor. A split second later, he did.

Boyd's bullet smashed into his forehead and then he saw nothing at all.

Ned Tanner fell, a puppet with its strings cut. In the middle of his forehead was the third eye opened by the bullet.

He didn't pull the triggers as he fell not even in reflex. All the strings were cut.

The hand cannon went off when it struck the floor, loosing one barrel. The blast blew a blackened hole in the floorboards, the edges burning. A haze of gun-smoke hovered a few feet above the floor.

Baldy looked back once before making his getaway into the fireplace. This time Boyd was sure that he was sneering.

Boyd angled for a shot, but it looked chancy. He rose on one knee, determined to risk it.

Baldy ducked into the passageway, carrying Mora. She was stunned, helpless—but alive.

Boyd rose, rushing the fireplace.

A *thunk!* sounded, followed by a *snick*.

The first came from within the fireplace, the second

seemed to have been struck by the cabinet clock.

The stone panel rumbled shut. Boyd got a final glimpse of Mora's face, piteous and despairing as darkness engulfed her.

Eight

Carr was dead. He lay crumpled on the tracks, between the baggage car and the private car. His head was twisted so his face was turned rearward. His expression was grotesque. His neck seemed to be covered with one enormous purple bruise.

The corpse was sprinkled with broken glass. The shards reflected the wan light leaking from behind the curtain covering the broken windows of the private car.

Megrim and Boyd stood looking at the body. A railroad car stood between them and the station.

The front door of the station was wide open. Light from inside fanned through the doorway and halfway across the boarding platform. It was a dark, damp, three o'clock in the morning.

"Wrung his neck like a chicken's," Boyd said. "And Carr was a big man."

"You should've seen the thing what done it to him," Megrim said.

"You saw it?" Boyd said.

"Yes, and I wish I hadn't. Lord! It was something," Megrim said. "At first, I thought it was a bear standing on its hind legs."

"What happened, Megrim?"

"It was Carr's turn on duty—a little while ago, not more than fifteen, twenty minutes ago. He was out walking patrol. Holtz and I were locked in the car, sleeping. I was kind of sleeping light. I'd heard noises earler."

"What kind of noises?"

"Nothing much. Sounds coming from under the train every once in a while. Train makes a lot of noises, even when it's standing still. Settling on its frame, the metal cooling . . . You can't get up and look every time you hear a noise, otherwise you'll be hopping up and down all night like a damned jack-rabbit.

"Besides, that's what the man on patrol is for. It's his job to investigate suspicious noises."

"I guess Carr found one," Boyd said.

"He was dead when I saw him," Megrim said.

"When was that?"

"About a minute after the shots went off in the station," Megrim said.

"*After* the shots?"

"Yes. Like I said, I was sleeping light. I heard what sounded like shots. That woke me up. Holtz, too," Megrim said.

He went on, "I heard something moving outside. It came up the steps to the platform. There was a banging on the door. Through the window at the top of the door I could see Carr.

"The door was locked. The man inside holds the key to the private car, as a safety measure. If something happens to the man outside, the key is still here and the door stays locked."

"Makes sense," Boyd said.

"It did this time. When I saw Carr, I knew he was dead. His face was pressed up against the glass, like he was standing there, but his eyes were rolled up in his head and his mouth was hanging open and there was no way he wasn't dead. There was a pounding on the door and the knob rattled. It got worse, as if Carr was getting mad that the door wouldn't open.

"I came up on the glass from below, edging up to the door with my head down, to keep from getting it blown off. I peeked around the corner of the frame, seeing past Carr to what had a hold of him.

"It was standing crouched over to one side of the door, trying to hide. As if you could hide something like that. Ha ha!"

Megrim's laughter was shaky. He may have realized that himself, for he quickly choked it off.

He began earnestly, "Listen, McMasters, I know it sounds crazy—"

"Nothing would surprise me in this madhouse," Boyd said.

"I thought it was a bear," Megrim said. "That's what I thought at first. But it wasn't. It was a big, hairy man—a huge, hulking brute!

"He had long shaggy hair, a beard, hair all over

his body . . . He was huge. He had a hold of Carr by the back of the neck, holding him up with one hand. Carr weighed over two hundred and twenty pounds!

"He saw me looking at him—the brute, that is. Carr was dead. You should've seen the look he gave me! Like an animal!"

Megrim shuddered. "He got mad then. He put Carr headfirst through the window, smashing the glass. He reached in, almost got me. Would have, if I hadn't jumped back so far I fell on my ass on the floor.

"Then the shooting started. The brute wasn't alone. He must have had at least one other working with him, a shooter. He cut loose, shooting through the windows. Me and Holtz were on the floor. When the shooting stopped, the brute man had gotten away. The shooter, too.

"Not that I was rushing out there after them," Megrim added, with a grin.

"There isn't much more to tell," he said. "Me and Holtz sat tight. There was more shooting in the station—that was your bit. You and Stubbs came out, Brown and Henshaw turned out to be okay, and here we are.

"My question is, what the hell are we doing here?"

"Business," Boyd said. "We're doing business."

Megrim scratched his head. "I don't follow."

"You're a train guard."

"So?"

"Well, the station is railroad property, ain't it?" Boyd demanded.

"I've got a feeling it's going to be under new management soon," Megrim said.

"There's liable to be a vacancy in the guard department, too, and I don't mean Carr."

Megrim's eyes narrowed. "What do you mean?"

"Foxes have been in the henhouse," Boyd said. "The baggage car's been robbed."

The baggage car's left side door was open.

"I've already been inside," Boyd said. "The body's gone. The body of their own, that is. The girl's body was left behind. They don't care who finds her.

"They got in using Carr's key. Attacking the private car was a diversion, a lure to hide what they were really after. Probably carried away the body under cover of the shooting."

"Cunning devils! Who are they, McMasters?"

"The Hell Killers," Boyd said.

"What do they want with the body? Why's it so important to them?"

"Maybe they don't like leaving any tracks."

"What good is that? Even if they steal the corpse, we've seen it . . ."

Megrim's voice trailed off.

"You get the idea," Boyd said. "Now we qualify as tracks."

Megrim looked around, straining to penetrate the darkness.

"Do we have to stand around out here, in the open?" he said.

"No. We'll go in and make plans," Boyd said.

They went to the private car. "What'll we do with him?" Megrim said, meaning Carr.

"We'll move him later," Boyd said.

They climbed the steps to the platform and entered the private car. The others were inside. Brown's head was bandaged, a dull red stain showing near the crown. Over it he wore a stiff-billed dark blue conductor's cap. He was loading a six-gun. Stubbs sat nearby, a rifle across his knees. Holtz knelt, looking out a corner of a window at the station.

At the rear of the car, Henshaw sat in the shadows, peering over the sights of a rifle whose barrel rested on the sill of the open window and was pointed at the station door.

"Anything moving in there?" Boyd said.

"Not a thing," Henshaw said.

"Well, if anybody in there wants to shut that door, they'll have to step outside," Boyd said.

"Not that it'll do them any good, since I jammed the lock and threw away the bar," he added.

"Let 'em try," Henshaw said. He looked up with a scowling grin. "They had their fun shooting at me and Brown in the caboose. Now it's my turn."

He returned to his vigil.

Megrim fidgeted. "I say we get out of here!"

"I agree," Stubbs said. He half rose, realized he was outlined against a shaded window, and sat back down.

"Let's git while the gittin's good," he said.

He leaned forward, as if to be closer to the door when the time came to move out.

"That might be just what they're waiting for us to do," Henshaw called down the aisle. "Make a run for it so they can cut us down."

"We can't stay here," Stubbs said.

"Attacking the railroad!" Brown sputtered, aghast at the effrontery of it all. "They must be insane!"

Boyd reloaded his guns and holstered them. He stuck two more guns in the top of his pants. From a weapons locker, he broke out a double-barreled sawed-off shotgun with a curved butt and chopped stock. He filled his pockets with shotgun shells.

He strapped on a knife with a foot-long blade, wickedly gleaming and razor-sharp. He wore it in a sheath hung under his left arm, secured by shoulder straps.

He found a box of matches and a tin of flammable liquid naphtha and some rags. He put the tin and the rags in a pouch that was sealed at the top by drawstrings. He tied the top of it to his belt, on his left hip. He buttoned the matches into a breast pocket of his shirt.

On a train there was no shortage of railroad lanterns. He took a lamp that was filled with oil.

He went to the door.

"Where you going?" Megrim said.

"The station," Boyd said.

"What for?"

"The girl."

People started shouting different things at once. As soon as there was a lull, Boyd said, "I'm going."

That triggered another round.

"She's dead!" Stubbs said.

"Hell, she's one of 'em," Henshaw said.

"She tried to warn me about old Ned. That'll go hard with her," Boyd said.

"She's a Tanner," Stubbs said.

"To hell with her," Megrim said.

Boyd looked surprised. "I don't recall asking for any help. Do what you like. I will."

"If you want to get killed, go ahead," Megrim said. "The rest of us have more sense."

Stubbs was fretful. "You put me in a spot," he said. "You saved my life. I owe you."

"Don't pay no nevermind to that," Boyd said. "It ain't nothing."

"Why throw your life away for that little Tanner bitch? She's not worth it. She's in it with the rest of them."

"I don't think so," Boyd said. "Her face, the way she looked when the wall closed, like she was being buried alive . . ."

"Better her than us," Megrim said. "Start the train, Stubbs."

Brown laughed, a mocking caw. Megrim stared

at him as though Brown had taken leave of his senses.

"How about it, Stubbs?" he said.

The engineer smiled grimly. "It ain't that easy, sonny. The boiler's got to be fired up to a full head of steam. That takes time."

"Right. I forgot." Megrim took off his hat, nervously smoothing his hair with his hand. "Get to firing her up. Sooner started, sooner done.

"Sooner gone," he added.

Brown vented another contemptuous hoot. "Haw! Losing his guts!"

Megrim turned on him angrily. "Shut up, old man!"

Stubbs started out of his seat, his hand raised for cuffing. Megrim cowered, throwing his hands in front of his face.

"You shut up," Stubbs said. "Who-the-hell-do-you-think-you-are, you piece of trash, mouthing off to Mr. Brown like that! He's the *conductor* of this train!"

He sat down heavily.

From the back of the train, Henshaw said, "Wonder if Carr was really dead when Megrim said he was."

"He was!" Megrim shouted. "Ask Holtz. He saw him too!"

"He sure looked dead," Holtz said.

"Just asking," Henshaw said.

Dawning comprehension showed on Megrim's face. "So that's it. I'm the heavy. I'm the bad guy for saying what we're all thinking: that we should save our skins."

"You talk too much," Stubbs said.

"Yeah? I don't see any of you going with Mc-Masters," Megrim said.

"Where'd he go?" Holtz said.

"He must've slipped out while we were jawing," Henshaw said.

Boyd was gone.

Nine

"You got guts," Henshaw said. Having caught up to Boyd, he stood shaking his head admiringly.

"I've got a plan," Boyd said.

Henshaw snorted. "Oh, yeah? What?"

"Now that I've got the enemy in one place, I'm going to go clean up on them," Boyd said.

"Save your breath, Henshaw," Brown said. "You can't talk him out of it. He's muleheaded."

"The mule'd have to kick me in the head before I'd go," Henshaw said, "and maybe not even then."

They were in the station, in the big room, a few minutes after Boyd had gotten off the train. Henshaw held a rifle. A gun was tucked in his belt. Brown wore a sidegun. He was tricked out in a fancy rig with a Sam Browne belt and a service revolver worn high on the hip. The holster flap was unbuttoned, and his hand rested on the gun butt. A general air of spiffiness hung over him. Even the bloodstain on his bandaged head was a neat red blotch.

Boyd toed a messier stain on the floorboards, where the dwarf, Pye, had breathed his last.

"Here's where I killed the dwarf," Boyd said. "They must've taken him away before carrying off the girl."

"They left Tanner," Henshaw said.

Ned Tanner lay where Boyd had shot him, sprawled on the floor like a carcass washed up on a beach.

Brown paced restlessly up and down the length of the big room, constantly going to the main hall to check that no lurkers were skulking in the corridors, then rejoining Henshaw and Boyd by the fireplace.

Henshaw rapped the slablike mantel stone with his knuckles and winced. "Ow. This thing's solid. If there's a hidden catch, it's hidden good. How are you going to get in? Looks like they jumped in a hole and pulled it shut after them."

"There's a way to open it from the other side, I know that," Boyd said. "There should be a way to open it from this side, and I think I know where it is."

He crossed to the cabinet clock. "Both times the secret door was in operation, there was a funny noise from over here, kind of like a gear setting or a catch being tripped. It could be some kind of apparatus used to reset the mechanism after each use—but why over here? Maybe because it's the control that opens the door from out here."

He ran his fingers over the cabinet, along the straight edges and the sculpted carvings, feeling for looseness, false panels, concealed studs. Glancing downward, he saw something that caught his eye. He left off his gropings, going down to one knee beside the cabinet.

"Um," he said.

Henshaw and Brown came over to see what he was doing.

At the bottom of the cabinet's front, the corner edge of the left panel was not entirely flush with the side rail but protruded forward about an eighth of an inch.

Boyd tried to get his fingernails under it, but he couldn't. He drew the long knife from its sheath, and Brown and Henshaw stepped back as the blade was freed.

"Somebody watch that we don't get sneaked up on," Boyd said.

Drawing himself up, Brown folded his arms across his chest, assuming a posture of keen-eyed vigilance. He placed himself with his back to the corner where the right rear wall met the long wall. From there, his angle of vision encompassed fireplace, big room, and the wall beyond. He rocked back and forth on his heels.

Boyd pressed the tip of the knife under the tiny projection at the base of the cabinet.

"Somebody was in a hurry and didn't shut it all the way," he said.

He wedged the corner nub farther out of its frame.

"Ah! Got it," he said.

At the bottom front of the cabinet were two re-

cessed decorative panels, tall and narrow. The left
panel was hinged on one side, opening to the right.

Henshaw grunted, craning for a better look over
Boyd's shoulder. The interior of the cabinet was laid
bare, a tangle of rods, levers, gears, and chains.

"This stuff's junk," Boyd said dismissively.
"Rusted solid."

He sheathed the knife, lit a match, and peered into
the interior.

"Don't want to go sticking my hand in a bear
trap," he said. "Hm, here's something . . ."

The match burned down, Boyd shedding it before
it could burn his fingers.

"There's a handle on the floor, under the machinery," he said. "That must be it."

He stood up. "If it works, I'm going in. So I'd
better get set."

He lit the railroad lantern. He checked to make sure
that his gear and hardware were secure.

He saw Henshaw speculatively eyeing the whiskey
bottle on the table. Henshaw reached for it.

"I'll drink to your luck," he said, raising the neck
to his lips.

"Don't!" Boyd said.

Alerted by the other's tone, Henshaw froze.

"It's drugged," Boyd said. "Specialty of the
house. Tanner left it for me, hoping I'd drink some.
I only had a taste and spoiled his plans.

"In case that didn't work, he shaved the odds some
more by giving me a shotgun that wouldn't fire. It

was gimmicked to fail. Made a good club, though,''
he said.

Henshaw looked at the bottle in his hand, then
threw it away. It hit the floor but didn't break, rolling
back and forth in a half-circle until it ran out of momentum and lay still.

Brown said, ''Wonder how many other travelers
took a drink like that and never woke up?''

''Good question,'' Henshaw said. ''Tanners've
been running this place for as long as I've been on
the line, and that's close to ten years.''

''They've been here longer than that,'' Brown said.
''Old Ned ran the place even before the railroad came
through, back when the wagon trains traveled the
pass. Wonder how many settlers died here, too?''

''The pass has always had a rep as a hard-luck
place,'' Henshaw said. ''Maybe that's why. The station's a perfect setup for a gang of robbers and killers.''

''It's made for murder,'' Boyd said. ''The secret
passages prove it. This was a fort once, back in the
days of the mountain men. The fur traders must have
dug tunnels as bolt-holes to escape the Indians if they
ever succeeded in storming the place.

''That's how the enemy is able to pass through
locked doors in and out of the station. The station
itself is honeycombed with secret passages. Convenient for slipping into a room at night and cutting
someone's throat without disturbing the other
guests.''

''It's a slaughterhouse,'' Brown said tartly.

Henshaw, thoughtful, rubbed his chin. "When you said 'mountain men,' you reminded me of something. The ones we drove off from the caboose, Brownie, didn't they kind of look like mountain men?"

"They looked like a pack of mad dogs," Brown said. "I still don't see how I missed when I shot at them."

"They was fast. But think about it, Brownie. They looked like those trappers you see sometimes in town, when they come in after a year or two in the wilderness. Smelled like it, too."

Brown pursed his lips. "I only got a glimpse of them, but there's something to what you say. I saw enough to know they were wild men."

Drawing himself up with dignity, he said, "That's *Mr. Brown* to you, Henshaw. Let's not forgo the formalities."

"He's a corker, ain't he?" Henshaw said.

"I'm ready," Boyd said. He was on one knee beside the cabinet. "Cover the fireplace while I throw the switch. They might be right on the other side of the wall. If they are, shoot first."

Brown and Henshaw got into position, guns aimed at the hearth. Brown stood on the left, arm holding the gun extended straight out, left hand held behind his back, body tilted at an angle to the fireplace. He looked like he was taking target practice at a shooting range.

On the right, Henshaw held his rifle leveled, hip-high. He and Brown stood apart, leaving Boyd, at the clock, a clear sightline and line of fire to the hearth.

In the cabinet, a metal plate, a lump of black iron
the size and shape of a brick, was bolted to the floor.
It looked old, though not as old as the cabinet's useless clockwork mechanisms. Built into the top of the
plate was an iron rod in a slot groove. The rod lay all
the way over to the right. Wary of traps, Boyd
reached in with the knife, placing the thin upper edge
flat against the underside of the knobbed rod.

"Here she goes," Boyd said.

He lifted the lever, encountering a fair amount of
resistance as he pried it to an upright position. He
pushed it down to the left, so that it lay flat in the
groove.

Snick—the sound of a catch being tripped. Followed by *THUNK*, as the wall-panel release was
thrown.

Boyd sheathed the knife and rose as the stone panel
swung open. Beyond, blackness.

"I'll be damned," Henshaw said.

Brown danced into the hearth, leading with his gun.
The fire was long dead. Heaped in the center of the
floor was a mound of cool ashes.

"Looks empty," Brown said, in a stage whisper
made echoey by the portal.

"Careful, Brownie," Henshaw said. "These birds
are tricky."

But it was empty. Boyd stood at the threshold, lantern in one hand, sawed-off shotgun in the other.

"You know what to do," he said.

"Sit tight until daybreak," Henshaw said.

Brown nodded. "Starting up the train now would

give those devils the chance to pick us off one by one in the dark.''

"The others are forted up in the baggage car," Henshaw said.

"Good place for a stand," Boyd said. "It's built to resist bandits, and the weapons are there."

"Too bad it don't lock."

"Oh, it locks, all right. Trouble is, the enemy has the keys," Boyd said. "Still, it's the safest place on the train."

"Stubbs, Megrim, and the kid can hold it by themselves. They'll have to. Me and Brownie'll wait here for you."

"Thanks," Boyd said. "If I'm not back by dawn, clear out. Don't wait, don't look for me, don't bother with the horses out in the barn. Get that train out of here and don't stop rolling until you reach Dunne at Three Forks."

Not waiting for a reply, Boyd ducked under the mantel, into the hearth, through the secret passage.

Ten

In the close air of the compartment, there was a smell of fresh blood, sharp and metallic. Also a pungent, musky man-stink. Boyd stood on the landing, facing the portal, lantern held shoulder high. He ran his fingers along the stones of the door frame, testing them for unusual features that might betray the location of a switch. Finding nothing, he examined the wall to the right of the door.

Away from the tightly fitted door frame, the stones were rougher, more irregularly shaped, gnarly.

Beyond the portal, he could see Brown and Henshaw, their faces anxious.

Boyd felt up and down the wall.

"You okay?" Henshaw said in a low voice.

"I'm looking for the control on this side," Boyd said out of the corner of his mouth. "Wait a minute—"

Reaching under a fist-size stone knob, his fingers touched hard-edged metal. Holding the lantern so he could see better, he peered up under the knob. It had been hollowed out, serving as a protective shield over the lever.

"Got it," Boyd said.

With his knife, he scratched a star-shaped marker into the stone above the knob.

"I'm not going to mess with it now, but I might need it later," he said.

Henshaw stuck his face in the portal, grinning. "You mean like if something should happen to me and Brownie?"

"I didn't even think of that," Boyd lied. "They might be able to close the door from below, though."

"Watch your backs. The way this place is rigged, trouble could come from any direction."

"Me and Brownie'll shoot their eyes out," Henshaw said. "Well, don't get killed."

"That's always the plan," Boyd said.

He turned, went to the top of the stairs. They were narrow, made, like the well walls, of fitted masonry stones. He held the lantern high. It cast a spidery ring of light around the circular shaft.

On the landing and the stairs were bloodstains, still wet. The dwarf's? Or Mora's?

Boyd adjusted the lamp, dimming it. The light web dulled, dwindling, supplanted by shadows. The shadows were thick, sludgy, like river-bottom muck.

Below, in the well, was a faint glow.

Boyd started downward, his shoulder brushing the curved wall. The stairs were little wider than his shoulders. On the inside curve there was no rail, nothing between the edge of the stairs and the well.

The ring of lantern light crept down the shaft, stone walls rising around Boyd. The rocks were damp—with moisture, he hoped. The stairs were slick, slippery. He stepped with care.

There were no cobwebs, not surprising in light of the recent traffic here. The well smelled like a combination sewer, swamp, and snakepit, and the odor got worse with each step downward.

Below, the top of an archway came into view. He was near the bottom of the shaft. It was only twenty or so feet below the landing, but darkness and the constricting spiral staircase had made it seem much deeper.

Boyd carefully set the lantern down on a step, its dimly lit globe a pale moon. The sole exit from the shaft was the archway. He crept to it, then boldly stepped through, into another stairwell.

The stones here were different, darker, more massive. He guessed that these were the original foundation stones laid down by the fur traders over a century ago. Patches of brown and black lichen clung to the liver-colored blocks.

Boyd got the lantern and started down the stairs. The shaft was not spiral but square-edged, the stones very rough. The air was bad.

Three steps down, the stairway made an *L*, then three more steps, then another *L*. Here the steps ran out. The last set of steps was different from the ones above. It was carved from the living rock, a dark gray clayey limestone.

At the bottom was a tunnel mouth, six feet high

and four feet wide. It looked like a natural fissure that had been made into a tunnel. The walls glowed dimly. At first Boyd thought the glow was from a light shining through the other end, then he realized that it was the walls themselves that were glowing. They were covered with palely luminous fungi that shone like fox fire. Dark patches and streaks showed where passersby had brushed the walls. No fungi grew on the tunnel floor walkway.

Boyd ducked his head to get through the tunnel. It was short, about ten feet long, opening into the stone room of a cave. It was a small cave, about the size of a one-room shack, the first of what appeared to be a series of caverns. Walls and ceiling were lined with more of the phosphorescent fungi. Without the lantern, dim though it was, he would not have been able to make his way.

Small stalactites hung from the ceiling, which was high enough for him to walk upright without hitting his head. The floor was slimed with several inches of gray-black muck. In the center of the space planks had been laid down for a walkway. On the sides were old packing crates, boards, mounds of refuse, a coil of frayed rope.

The air was better here. It smelled worse, but at least it was moving. A natural ventilating system kept the air circulating through the caverns.

At the far end of the cave, a gallery wormed through the rock, making a sharp turn every half-dozen paces or so.

The walls were narrow, slick, confining. Boyd felt

as if he were crawling through the guts of some giant animal.

Ahead, light. He neared the end of the gallery. Hugging the rock, he peeked around the edge.

Beyond lay a cavern, vast and gloomy, thick with shadows. It was shaped like a covered dish. The shallow bowl floor was as big across as a dance floor. The dome-shaped ceiling was thirty feet tall at its highest. In some places, stalactites growing down and stalagmites growing up joined, forming twisted columns that spanned ceiling and floor.

Stone surfaces were damp, glistening. They seemed not so much mineral as organic. The luminous fungi seemed banished to the far corners of the space, like an outbreak of mange.

Curtains of mist hung in midair, shot through with lurid gleams of firelight. Titan shadows flickered on the walls. There was the sound of running water.

Rock outcroppings dotted the floor, breaking the space up into a maze of smaller sections, some connected, others not.

There were voices, shapes.

A scream. Mora's?

Boyd couldn't see what was happening. He set aside the lantern, its wan glow drowned by the cavern's smoky light.

He crept out from behind the rock.

Standing little more than an arm's length away was an Enemy, a spindly figure slouching in stinking buckskins.

A mass of long, greasy, black hair, marbled with

white, hung down to the small of the Enemy's back, which was turned to Boyd. Puffing on a corncob pipe, the Enemy rested a hand on the muzzle of a rifle that was held upright, its butt grounded on the floor. The Enemy wore a sidegun and a belt knife. Decorative fringe trimmed the buckskins, hanging down like strands of snot.

More screams.

The Enemy craned, trying to see the fun. Boyd thought his approach was noiseless, but the other, warned by some sixth sense, started to turn away.

Boyd came up behind the other, hooked his left arm around a neck, held the head, and twisted sharply.

The other's frantic struggle lasted only as long as it took to break her neck, a split second.

A timely scream drowned the sound of snapping bone.

Boyd gave the now-slack head an extra-vicious twist to finish the job. He steadied the rifle, catching it before it could fall from a dead hand.

The pipe hit the floor, spilling hot ashes.

Boyd dragged the body to the side, behind a rock. The corpse had a wizened face, dark eyes glaring insanely from out of a nest of wrinkles, tongue lolling from between near-toothless gums.

Boyd wiped his hands on his pants. He disabled her rifle and laid it beside her. He wiped his hands again.

He moved forward, working his way through the rocks. On both sides, the cave was ridged with rock ribs thrusting up from the floor, highest where the floor met the ceiling and lowest in the center aisle. It was impossible to walk across the middle of the floor without having to go over or around a rock. The formation created a number of bays, or coves, open sections ringed by rings into semi-private subsections. Some of these had been partitioned into walled enclosures. One was filled with casks and barrels, stacked into piles. Another was floored with furs and blankets, apparently a sleeping place, now dark, empty. A third held lumber, planks, boards, beams, and odd-shaped fragments, all heaped together.

Boyd followed a winding route to avoid being seen. He had to make some wide detours, wandering through a cluster of partitioned walls.

A three-sided stall held clothes, a wide variety of garments: men's and women's, children's. There were coats and jackets, shirts, piles of trousers, mounds of shoes.

His path took him way over to the left of the cavern. Each time he tried to angle back toward the center, a new wall blocked him, forcing him still farther to the side.

One turning led him to a wide oval of open floor butted up next to the cavern wall, enclosed between a pair of rock ribs. On the right an eight-foot-high wooden-post fence screened off the center of the cave.

It was a kind of butcher shop–storeroom. In the middle of the space stood a flattopped rock as big as a billiards table. Carved into the top were grooves for draining blood. A scarred wooden bench table lined a nearby wall. On it, in varying states of filth, were saws, knives, cleavers, and other instruments of the butcher's trade.

Around the stone slab had been erected a wooden-frame scaffolding of beams and cross-braces. Hanging on hooks from the long top poles were sides of meat, limbless gutted carcasses, some quite gamy.

Boyd tried to remember what he had eaten for dinner. There hadn't been much meat in the stew, but he was pretty sure it had been beef.

This wasn't.

He recalled the girl on the trail, the one who had been killed by Scarecrow what seemed ages ago but in reality only two days previously.

On her flesh, on breasts and belly and hindquarters and haunches, she had borne the almost unbelievable stigma of fiendish depravity: human bite marks.

They were by-products of sadistic sexual frenzy and torture. What confronted him in the butcher stall was worse. It was efficient. It was systematic. It was meat.

That's what people were to the Hell Killers.

Just meat.

He'd heard of such things—rumors, always told of shadowy figures and faraway climes. The Apache war chief who devoured, steaming, the still-beating heart torn from the chest of a foe. The pirate who cut off a victim's ears, fried them, and ate them for breakfast. The Mexican bandit with a golden cup for drinking his victims' lifeblood.

Less shadowy was the Donner party, snowbound settlers trapped in a mountain pass for the winter, with no food but the dead. The French seamen marooned on the raft of the ship *Medusa*, forced into cannibalism to survive. There was the well-documented fact that, throughout history, certain citizens of besieged cities waxed fat while their fellows died of famine.

This was different. It was real.

Not only butchering, but smoking and curing had taken place here as well. There were hogsheads of briny pickling solution, things floating in them. There were hair and bones and gristle and offal.

A shelf held a row of heads floating in fluid-filled glass jars.

In a corner, swept neatly by a straw broom that was kept for that purpose, was a pile of clean-picked bones.

The stall was alive with crawling things, vermin.

Suddenly saving the girl didn't seem as important as not being eaten himself.

Remembering the tin of naphtha, Boyd took heart. *I'll burn first.*

No, he corrected. *They will.*

He eased toward the slanted wall, moving more stealthily than he had before finding the butcher stall. That was no good. How long before the missing sentry was noticed?

The slanted wall stood between Boyd and the center zone. Light slanted through the cracks between the upright posts. He peered through them.

The enemy clustered around the girl. There was Baldy, who had carried her off. There was a bird-faced old hag. There was a gold-toothed lad in a jacket with a wolf-fur collar. There was a young cowboy with an open face and a sweet smile.

A handful of others were in the background, vague shapes.

In the foreground stood Mora Tanner. Her nightgown was shredded, a filthy rag. She screamed in an extremity of madness and terror.

The cowboy stood behind her, holding her wrists, smiling.

The hag poked the girl's soft parts with the sharp end of a stick. The cowboy's smile widened.

To the left, apart from the others, stood a man on a rock that placed his feet above their heads. He postured in a stance of extreme dominance. His head was tossed back, his fists were on his hips, and his feet were planted wide apart.

He was past his prime, slightly gone to seed. His hair was slicked back straight from the forehead. Except for a touch of gray at the temples, it was oxblood color, the same color shared to a greater or lesser degree by all the Tanners.

He could have been the middle sibling between Ned and Kate Tanner.

Come to think it, most of the group on the cavern floor were touched by the traits of what could be called the "Tanner look."

A lot of oxblood-colored scalps—except for Baldy's, of course. Even Mora's hair was a pale variant of that same hue.

Below the man on the rock, on a lower ledge, lay the body of Pye, the dwarf.

The man on the rock motioned for silence. The hag, oblivious, continued to torment Mora.

The man said, "Blaze."

Blaze was the name of the man that Boyd called, "Baldy." He seemed to be the second in command of the man on the rock.

The hag, realizing she'd done wrong, cowered. Blaze punched her in the back. She bowed outward, falling forward in a painful heap, biting off a yelp.

That got a laugh from some of the others.

Blaze leaned forward, thrusting his face close to the hag's.

"When Arkon talks, listen!" he said.

"B-but he didn't say anything," the hag said, confused.

Blaze backhanded her to the floor. "Listen anyway!"

He stepped forward to kick her, falling back when Arkon signaled him to desist.

"We're shorthanded now," Arkon said, deep-voiced.

"Bah! She's useless anyhow," Blaze said.

A suspicion of worry creased the young cowboy's open, guileless face. "What about the others? They're coming, ain't they?"

"They're a long way off, Jerry," Arkon said gently. "They may not arrive in time."

"Shucks," Jerry said, pouting.

"I'm sure we can handle things ourselves."

"Now you're talking," Blaze said. When he got excited, his bald scalp flushed a deep red.

"Let's go up and kill those outsiders," he said.

He drew a knife that resembled a black iron spear blade and waved it in front of Mora's face.

"We'll start on this outsider first," he said.

The gold-toothed lad stopped chewing on a toothpick long enough to remark, "She ain't an outsider, she's family."

"No!" Mora shrieked.

Blaze looked up triumphantly. "See? She's got no use for her own kind."

"She's tetched," Jerry said, tapping the side of his head. "She can't think straight, like the rest of us."

"She's weak," Blaze snapped. "Worse, she's a traitor. She tried to warn the meat-men. She must die!"

"That's a waste of good breeding stock," Gold-tooth said.

"I know what you want her for, Fenris!" Blaze said, sneering.

Gold-toothed Fenris shrugged. "She's got the family bloodline. She's weak, but her whelps may be strong."

Jerry hitched up his pants. "Shoot, I wouldn't mind taking a crack at her myself."

"Well, Arkon?" Blaze said. "What's it to be?"

Arkon rested his head in his hand, and his elbow in the palm of his other hand, studying the question.

"A-hem," he said at last. "A knotty problem. Ordinarily, I'd try to save the bloodline, but these are extraordinary times. It'll be all we can do to save ourselves. After we destroy all traces of our existence here, we must go far, far away.''

"Back to the northern mountains?'' the hag qua-vered.

"If necessary,'' Arkon said.

Fenris spoke out. "We were starving up there. If we go back, we'll starve again. Here there's food, liquor, and females!''

"What good are they when you're dead? The meat-men have the scent of us now. Alone, they're insects, but once they get organized, they're formidable!''

Jerry looked as if he was going to cry.

"Is it too late for a getaway?'' he asked.

"No,'' Arkon said. "Not if the outsiders who have learned of us are dead.''

"What are we waiting for? Let's go get them,'' Fenris said.

"Wait!'' Blaze grabbed the hair at the top of Mo-ra's head, twisting it, making her squirm.

"What about her, Arkon? Say the word—and make it *death*,'' Blaze said.

"It was an experiment,'' Arkon said. "Brother Ned and Sister Kate raised the girl in ignorance of her heritage. It couldn't be helped. The father was a meat-man, the mother was one of us. She died in a mad-house after birthing the girl. Sister Kate claimed her, raising her a thousand miles from here, in a city on the plain. To live among the fold, you must act like a sheep. By the time Sister Kate brought the girl back home to the valley, the damage was done. Believing herself a sheep, the girl had a horror of us.

"She also suffers from the strain of hereditary insanity in the family bloodline, the same mental weakness that caused her natural mother to scream out her life in an insane asylum. Were we so foolish as to spare her, we'd soon find ourselves saddled with a hopeless lunatic. Indeed, I fear she may already have gone stark, raving mad. It's a mercy to release such a poor, deluded soul.''

Arkon nodded. ''You may do the honors, Blaze, my boy.''

He looked sad, sounded sad. Blaze raised the knife.

Mora shrieked, the scream of a madwoman.

Jerry frowned, sniffing.

''I smell smoke,'' he said.

Eleven

"Fire, fire!"

The fire was good and hot. Boyd had splashed plenty of the highly inflammable naphtha fluid all over the butcher stall, then touched it off with a match.

With a *whoomph!* a disk of ghostly blue flames expanded outward from the flash point, like ripples when a rock is dropped in a pond. Flames leaped up, yellow and red, scribbling fire across the walls, tables, shelves.

In seconds it was a mini-inferno, venting heat, light, and smoke.

There was lots of shouting.

With the chaos going good, Boyd stepped out from behind the wall, into the inner circle.

The sawed-off shotgun belched fire and smoke, a tremendous single-barreled blast.

Blaze's head exploded like a melon struck by a sledgehammer, spraying gore on those around him.

The second barrel was meant for Arkon. Too late, Boyd saw a figure looming over him, a man he'd failed to see behind the curve of a stone column.

A hairy man, looking like a bear standing on its hind legs. He was right on top of Boyd, open arms reaching out to crush him.

Boyd blasted him point-blank in the belly.

The hairy man hurtled backward.

Bullets popped around Boyd. Cowboy Jerry had dropped into a crouch with a six-gun, fanning. Slugs flew, missing Boyd. A stray tagged the crone, knocking her down.

Boyd dropped the empty shotgun, drawing a six-gun before it hit the ground. Before he could shoot, a bullet creased his left shoulder, spinning him so he fell.

Fenris was the one who had hit him. He looked capable. Firing from the floor, Boyd drilled him.

Fenris was hit in the middle. The impact paralyzed him. His face purpled. His mouth hung open. He tried to breathe, couldn't.

His legs folded. He dropped to his knees. Boyd shot him again. He fell forward.

The butcher stall was a mass of flame. Smoke thickened under the cave's roof.

Arkon jumped from rock to rock like a mountain goat, making for a bolt-hole high in the rear right wall of the cave. He climbed the rocks like steps, hurtling toward the hole.

Boyd shot him in midair, as he was leaping from one rock to another.

Arkon was hit in the leg. He screamed and dropped straight down, bouncing off ledges until he hit the floor. He didn't fall far, but he fell hard.

He fell behind a rock where Boyd couldn't see him.

Boyd rose up on his side. He tried his left arm, found he could move it. A deep crease. There was some numbness, and blood trickled down his arm.

He stood up, tilting to one side. The fire was roaring. It made a sound like a field full of flags whipping in a stiff breeze. It was eating up a lot of air. A lot of cave, too.

A figure rushed him, head down, bulling into him. The attacker came in low, shouldering Boyd's middle, sweeping him sideways into the blazing wall.

They bounced off, grappling, falling to the floor.

Boyd found himself face to face with Cowboy Jerry. He butted him, smashing the ridge of his crown square in the middle of the other's face, splashing his nose.

Jerry howled.

Boyd worked his gun hand free from Jerry's grip. He pressed the muzzle against the other's side and fired. Jerry jerked from the impact. Boyd pulled the trigger again, but the gun was empty.

He shrugged Jerry off, drew another gun, and shot him dead.

Thanks to the fire, there was plenty of light to see by, except that smoke got in the way. It was hard to breathe, too. The air was oven-hot.

The girl sprawled on the floor, not moving. Boyd staggered to her. Her eyes were closed. She lay gasping for breath. He grabbed her arm, shook her. She coughed but didn't move or open her eyes.

He tried to lift her but lacked the strength. If he could only rest for a moment . . .

Exhausted, he sat down on a rock, just for a second. He rubbed his eyes. They stung, teared. Smoke was getting to them.

From behind the other side of the rock, a hand reached up and stabbed him in the leg.

The knife was a long, slim dagger with a pearl handle. It was buried in the muscle of his right thigh.

He bellowed his pain and rage.

The hand pulled the knife out of his thigh. Blood jetted from the wound. The knife was in the hand of Arkon, crouched behind the rock.

Boyd's hand shot out, grasping the wrist of the knife hand. His other hand held a gun, whose barrel he whipped lickety-split across the side of Arkon's forehead.

He kept hitting him. Arkon slumped to the ground.

Boyd shot him through the chest.

Arkon kicked, spasming.

Boyd holstered his gun, took off the bandanna around his neck, and tied it over the wound in his thigh. He was lucky. The knife hadn't hit any arteries.

He was surprised to find the tin of naphtha still in his pocket, where he had thrust it after emptying most of its contents to start the blaze.

He shook the tin. There was still a little left, sloshing around inside. He unscrewed the cap and emptied it on Arkon.

In another minute, the fire would reach Arkon, setting him alight, but why should Boyd deny himself the pleasure?

He struck a match and flipped it on Arkon. Flames rose . . .

Boyd went to Mora. The wound in his thigh made him limp, but at least he could walk. Could he walk out with Mora? That remained to be seen.

He shook her, pulled her hair, slapped her face, anything to rouse her. Her flesh was cold, rigid. He raised her arm. When he let go, it stayed straight out.

He grasped her wrist, got his shoulder under her arm, and straightened his legs. The strain on his bad leg almost caused it to fold, but he fought through it and stayed on his feet.

She was on her feet, too. She moved like a sleepwalker, but at least she wasn't falling down.

They might make it out of here alive yet.

No doubt there were plenty of secret tunnels exiting the cave, but Boyd didn't know where they were and it was too late to start looking. If he got out at all, he'd get out the way he came.

Limping along, half-carrying Mora Tanner, he made his way across the cave floor toward the tunnel mouth on the other side.

Up popped a fiery phantom, from behind a rock.

The apparition was a man of flame, a human torch, a shambling grotesque glorified by the fiery fingers swathing him from head to toe.

Waving its arms, it lurched toward Boyd and the girl.

It was Arkon.

He staggered a few paces before the blackened sticks that were his legs crumbled, spilling him to the floor.

He lay there burning, his own funeral pyre.

"It's the Big Die-Up, pardner," Boyd said.

Mora's trance state was replaced by horrified delight. Her eyes bulged in wonderment. Her face shone. There was color in her cheeks, animation in her expression.

She covered her mouth with her hand.

A giggle escaped.

More followed, a fit of giggles. She sounded more than a little batty. The giggling got on Boyd's nerves. He thought about clipping her with the gun barrel, not hard, just a light tap behind the ear to stop the giggling.

But she moved along under her own power and didn't give him any trouble, so he resisted the impulse to clobber her.

Somehow they escaped.

Twelve

A column of black smoke marked the wreckage of Packer Point Station as the train rushed away from it, eastbound. Puffs of smoke jetted from the engine's stack. It was a clear blue-sky morning.

The train raced across the flat. Ahead lay Rainbow Gorge, its depths spanned by a trestle bridge. On the far side of the gap lay Three Forks crossing, where Dunne and company waited for the train.

In the private car, Boyd finished leafing through the documents and put them back in the folder.

Bleekman had taken out an insurance policy. Fearing at the last that he had bitten off more than he could chew in his attempt to blackmail Kate Tanner, he put the incriminating papers in a parcel package addressed to himself at a post office box in Virginia City. He had then given charge of the parcel over to Brown, whose duties encompassed railroad mail deliveries. He had thought this would give him an edge over Kate Tanner.

Later, after Boyd and Mora Tanner had emerged through the fireplace portal, coughing and choking, Henshaw and Brown helped them out of the station to the train.

Before the train got under way, Brown remembered the package and brought it forward.

The documents were police records and newspaper clippings relating to a "Merry Widow" killer who had operated in the Midwest, poisoning a series of husbands after first draining all their funds. The murders dated back fifteen years, coinciding with the period of Kate Tanner's wanderings from Shatter Valley.

Was she the poisoner? Bleekman seemed to think so.

"Poor Bleekman," Boyd said. "He thought he was dealing with an ordinary murderess. He must have suspected different, toward the end, when he realized that what he thought he had ahold of, had a hold on him."

"What about the girl?" Henshaw said.

"I don't know," Boyd said.

"She's nuts."

"Well . . ."

"She's crazy," Henshaw stated flatly. "She ought to be locked up in a lunatic asylum."

"It might come to that. I hope not. Maybe Doc Rhune can do something for her," Boyd said.

The others knew only the thinnest version of what had happened below. They knew nothing of the butcher stall. No one ever would, if Boyd could help it.

With any luck, the fire would have destroyed the evidence.

Henshaw scowled. "You're crazy yourself, letting that gal run around loose."

Boyd sat up straight. "*What*?"

"She needs a keeper," Henshaw said.

"No, no. What's that you said, about her running around loose?"

"Yeah."

"Can't be. She's sleeping on a back bunk."

"Oh, yeah? Take a look for yourself, pal," Henshaw said.

Boyd stood up, faltering for an instant when he put too much weight on his bad leg. He held a chair to steady himself. The train rushed on, rocketing down the rails, the car swaying from side to side with a rocking horse motion.

At the far end of the car, in the bunk where Mora Tanner had seemingly been sound asleep when Boyd had last glanced at her, only a few minutes ago, the blankets were thrown back and the mattress was empty.

Boyd said, "She didn't get past me."

"I came through the rear of the train and didn't see her," Henshaw said.

"Think she jumped off?"

"She might have. Who knows what a crazy person will do?"

The train sped up going into a curve, throwing

Boyd and Henshaw to one side.

"Keerist!" Henshaw said. "What's Stubbs thinking of, going this fast?!"

He peered through the window, looking ahead.

"This is the approach to the gorge! We've got to slow down, not speed up!" he said.

Scenery bulleted past.

Henshaw chewed his lip. "Stubbs must be out of his mind!"

"Not Stubbs!" Boyd shouted.

"You don't think—oh, God!"

In the engine cab, Holtz, who had been handling fireman chores, now lay curled on his side on the floor, trying to hold his guts in with both hands.

Stubbs cowered in a corner, face and hands slashed.

At the controls stood Mora Tanner, eyes alive with madness, brandishing a bloody knife. She did not work the controls, she merely ensured that no one else did.

The train chuted down the final downgrade, the intricate sticklike construction of the wooden trestle bridge fast approaching.

The train careened, seemingly about to jump the tracks at any second.

Scrambling up over the top of the tender car came Henshaw and Boyd, too late.

Stubbs looked up with sick eyes. "The throttle's wide open! We can't stop!"

"We're gonna crash!" Henshaw shouted. "Jump!"

"We're going too fast!" Boyd said.

The chasm neared. With a despairing cry, Henshaw leaped off the car and vanished.

Stubbs tried to crawl away. Quick as thought, Mora slashed him across the back, opening his flesh. Stubbs flopped on his belly, reaching behind him to clamp his hands on the wound.

The light had already gone out of Holtz's eyes.

Mora waved the knife, laughing.

Boyd got ready to jump. For an instant, he made eye contact with Mora.

"The Big Die-Up!" she screamed. "How do you like it?"

She held down the whistle as the train jumped the rails and nosed downward over the edge to oblivion.

J. L. REASONER

AUTHOR OF *RIVERS OF GOLD*

___*Healer's Calling*___   0-425-15487-4/$5.99

On the bloody battlefields of the Civil War,
Sara Black had proven her courage and skill
as a medic. Now, the war had ended, but she
had found her true calling: to become one of
America's first woman doctors.
(June '96)

___*The Healer's Road*___   0-515-11762-5/$5.99

When his parents died because of a lack of
proper medicine, Thomas Black vowed to
become a doctor and better people's lives.
Now, with the advent of war, he is challenged
to provide better care than ever before–in a
fraction of the time. During the savage conflict
of the Civil War, Thomas Black, and his two
children who follow in his footsteps, will embody
the true nobility of the American spirit.